ON

He sat with comfortable gr simply caressing the fur on the .... Alsatian, which sat upright and alert at his master's side. The softening alpine sunlight highlighted the deep thought in his brown eyes, pondering the next move in this monumental game of chess. With his aged thumb and index finger, he gently toyed with the small and always in-cheque moustache, perfectly central to his stern upper lip. The dark brown leather chair was situated in the centre of the vast, oversized and under-furnished room, ahead of the blazing fireplace, casting flickering shadows along the length of the room. He was wearing a suit cut to perfection, deep ocean in colour and pressed to form creases in all the right places. The shirt was a crisp white, like the ground atop the alpine hills, and he wore an emblem which sat neatly between the triangular gap created by the buttoned collar of the shirt.

"Keep the door closed!"

The visitor had barely set a foot in the room before the man uttered the words with the authority and conviction of all his moves. The door to the large sitting room was located behind the simple leather wingback chair; even though the visitor was out of sight and unable to make eye contact with the man, he gave a polite solute before fully committing to making his way towards the occupied chair. Despite there only being the two men in the room, the visitor delivered his message in a nervous whisper, his heart beating against his chest so loud he felt the need to raise his trembling voice, just a little, in order to be heard. Even before the message had been fully conveyed, the seated man's pupils dilated with a surge of adrenaline, his hearing muffled, mouth drier than the kindling lying next to the hearth; he sat forward ever so slightly, although he had the control to suppress any signs of anxiety to the intruder, ironing them into a seamless ballet of generic movements. With a sharp, almost over the top salute, the visitor left the room at once, having finished his delivery and not wanting to pester the man anymore.

He sank back into his chair. With new contemplation atop his next chess move now swirling around his exhausted mind, he felt like his head might sway slightly such was the weight of his thoughts. Hauling himself from the abraded seat, he shuffled to the drinks globe and refreshed his half-empty glass of Chilean red; the whole process performed with his rock steady right hand, while his left was tucked neatly behind his back and shaking steadily. Slowly, he made his way across the grand room to the even grander full height window, which created a mural painted with mountainous greys, snowy whites and dusk reds. Positioned exactly central to the window, he starred with a distant, unknowing gaze, almost looking through the vista, hoping to see something previously hidden. More than a number of moments passed, and his precision stance changed not once. With the eventual cessation of his trembling hand, he pressed it against the immaculate glass before continuing his hunched posture.

His tired eyes crawled their way across the landscape, and his hair, once black as night and groomed to perfection was beginning to show silver rivers and jagged faces. His breath, very deliberate and commanding, with a firm aroma of coffee, darted to the cooling window and just managed to form small tears of condensation, which trickled with a hasty nature to the oak crossbar of the frame. With the weight of a million men on his eyes, it took increasingly great effort to open his eyelids after each closure. He returned to the safety of his chair and fell heavily, such that the wine leapt from the crystal cut glass to find its ways to the polished parquet floor, adding to the numerous blood red spills.

A man in a pristine blue uniform entered the quiet and lonesome room, with a reserved confidence, trying not to seem overly brash in front of the man, who he had the utmost admiration for. A strong solute later, and the second visitor delivered his information, standing to the side of the armchair and not making eye contact, but looking straight and level at the wood panelling on the far wall. It was simply stated in a soft yet firm tone that there was an awaiting phone call for the man; there was a telephone in the room, but it never rang. All calls were intercepted and first screened, and only those deemed worthy would be able to speak with the man.

The messenger stood in silence and tugged at his peripheral vision to try and see the man's response. A simple nod conveyed that the message had been understood, and at the same time signalled for the intruder to leave the man's sanctuary. As quick as a solute, the messenger had left the room, and once more the man was all alone, except for his loyal dog. The dying flames of the fire cast dark, slowly waltzing shadows over the minimal obstacles in the room and the fast reducing luminosity barely trickled across the mill pond smooth flooring.

Once more the leather groaned as he pushed off the wearing arms of the chair to position himself upright, and made the almighty trek to the silent Bakelite handset, perched on a neat round table only just big enough, in a far corner. After what felt like the passage of an era, he found himself lifting the somewhat tired looking phone to his weary looking face, and although he knew the caller would know who *he* was, the man answered the phone in the way he always did, in his clear and dominant tone.

"Adolf Hitler sprechen…"

A message was relayed down the phone line. His tight eyelids scraped open in a single tired effort as his rich brown eyes dilated, opening like chasmal voids, drawing in the desperately retreating light.

TWO

A cymbal clash signified the falling of another mortar; if Sergeant Westfield had been trying to count the number that fell, each successive orchestral thud left him having to fight to regain focus. Fiercely trying to hold off advancing German forces flooding up through the narrow and ruined streets on the outskirts of Berlin, the small group of allied fighters were crouched in a crater dug out by the payload of a Lancaster bomber, which had reduced two of the surrounding buildings to little more than fine chalk dust. The sky was a steel grey, even the sun having taken flight from the scene. The impenetrable cold cloud cover was torn through with yet another mortar shell, shrieking to the earth before slamming into the ground. Each time the sequence appeared in slow motion; the mortar would disturb the rubble laden area, itself delivering an ample shock through the ground, throwing up a screen of hazy yellow dust; the detonation of the charge followed, firing fragmented casing along with a portion of the surrounding crumbling landscape in every possible direction, removing obstacles foolish enough to stand in the way; excess debris would fall back to the scarred land, settling for but a moment before it was to be disturbed once more.

Westfield shook his ringing head to overcome the shell shock, clutched his Sten sub-machine gun with white knuckles, gritted his dirty chipped teeth and opened fire over the top of their sheltering crater. The gun gave a rhythmic beating as it spat out spent golden cartridge cases down by the mud laden boots of a fallen comrade. The recoiling weapon snaked across the bullet riddled street, and his weathered hands had to tighten further to reign the uncontrollable beast. Incoming hand signals and facial contours conveyed that a Panther tank was approaching, and that the small group would have to move for the sake of self-preservation. Lined up like the start line of an olympic track, the group awaited the starting gun to signal the commencement of their race. Westfield reloaded his gun and was sitting low with his back against the lumpy sloped crater wall, his head just covered by the brim of the depression in the land. The detonation of a grenade thrown by the allied group leader, Captain Briggs, signalled for the men to sprint for their lives to the decaying shell of an unrecognisable building ahead and to the side of the crater. Westfield ripped the dog tags from the warm neck of the fallen gunner before jumping to his feet and firing upon the enemy while running for the new safe point; his dark brown hair danced and swayed as he ran, shedding days of dust and rubble, and the deep war beaten lines upon his face delivered painful leers towards his foe, while his war cry echoed with an almost musical tone to match the harmonious notes of all the explosions and gunfire from both ahead and behind. He darted into the ruined house to join his team, removing the exhausted magazine from the side of the gun and replacing it with a cool, fresh stack of pointed metal and gunpowder.

All fell silent. The crackle of gunfire and plodding of shells ceased the moment Westfield's foot set inside the house. He made a point of taking stock of the updated surroundings; a dusty, splintered wooden floor, half a rickety staircase leading up to a small remnant portion of first floor, just big enough for two men. There was a stone fireplace on the back wall, and a dark wooden bar situated on the far wall behind the men; the building had clearly once been an inn, and it seemed ironic to Westfield how in times of such despair it was able to function as a house of refuge, giving shelter from the storm outside. It was evident the place had been abandoned in a hurry, from the presence of tumbled tumblers strewn across the bar and disturbed decanters, still containing a multitude of different spirits spanning the entire spectrum of the rainbow. The fire had been snuffed out prematurely, probably with water administered by the dented galvanised bucket lying adjacent to the hearth. There was a half burnt log and some charred pages of newspaper resting on the fire grate.

A bang and thud of a shell from the Panther striking the adjacent building broke Westfield's foolishly meandering mind. The explosion removed the front of the hit building, tearing through the bricks and mortar as though they were wet newspaper. The allied fighters had positioned themselves at the windows throughout the inn, both on the ground floor and remainder of the first floor; Westfield took up position at the window next to the door, which was central to the front of the building. He cocked his weapon and lined up his eye with the two sighting pins atop the barrel; poised, he waited for an enemy soldier to come into view.

The Panther tank roared and the tracks squealed as the metallic monster lurched up the street, pursued by the German forces. The tank could not be seen from the inn as it was too far down the street, but each moment the high pitched and painful tone of the tank's movement got louder; it was as though a chalkboard were positioned adjacent Westfield's ear that someone was slowly running their nails down to make the most spine clenching and nerve twitching noise possible. He gritted his teeth and screwed up his already wrinkled face in a desperate attempt to hinder the excruciating attack on his ears. He lost focus and his vision blurred, enough for him to not realise the tank had crawled over all the pieces of glass, brick and bodies to come to rest right outside the inn. From the rear of the metallic monster, German forces began to emerge like ants from a disturbed nest. Both sides opened fire.

Westfield crouched behind the paint-peeling window frame and loosed off round after round, unsure which bullets were his through the fog-like spread of warm lead from both inside and outside of the inn. A German was finally hit; the bullet entered his right shoulder and exited via the middle of his back, bringing through with it a torrent of cherry red which graffitied the left hand panels of the pallid armour plating on the tank. The individual fell backwards, connecting the back of his head with the steel tank tracks before coming to rest, sitting upright leaning against the tank. He did not cry out in pain, but simply turned to his wound and stared, before raising his left hand to touch, in a manner of almost self-assurance, just to confirm what clearly was the case. The man's mouth was open, and a look upon his face of defeatist acceptance; saliva ran from the corner of his mouth onto the pale blue-green uniform, which was growing redder as it soaked up precious blood. He used all of his last remaining strength to lift his head, and simply looked at Westfield, with a distant yet questioning gaze that compelled Westfield to release his finger from the life taking trigger, and he then simply starred back at the unknown German soldier. The man's increasingly pale face started to quiver and his eyes were clearly becoming heavier. He cast his rifle aside with very exaggerated and staggered actions. He reached into the breast pocket of his uniform and retrieved a picture; slowly his deep gaze moved from Westfield to the photograph of his wife and daughter; he gave a slight smile as a single tear fell onto the dog-eared, black and white piece of card, and he lifted the photograph to his cold lips. A single bullet went ripping through the man's skull, before he had a chance to kiss goodbye his family, his head immediately dropped and he slumped over to one side, the warm stone of the dug up street to become his grave.

Westfield watched with horror before being shaken, and told to snap out of it. He shook his head and had a look of bewilderment upon his face, as though he had just awoken from a puzzling but somehow meaningful dream.

Once again he tightened his clasp on the sub-machine gun and opened fire into the hoard of Germans closing in on their position. The muzzle flash with each successive shot illuminated the dirty, adrenaline fuelled face, and a new light was cast as he became increasingly enraged, tensing his jaw and squinting just slightly in an attempt to better pin point where to direct the stream of lead. Enemy after enemy fell, accompanied by spurts and lacings, cries and yells, cheers and taunts.

The tank turret began to swing toward the inn, but was unable to direct its mighty barrel at the allies due the narrow streets and tall buildings impinging the movement. The small group barely noticed their good fortune as German soldiers kept advancing on their position. Despite the tank barrel coming to rest on a building two doors down form the inn, the gunner fired a shell, bringing the building to its knees in an instant; clumps of brick and mortar hurled down and struck the turret, sounding a resonant ping, before rolling off the tank gracefully to the disturbed, dusty ground. The cleared space allowed the lengthy barrel to move onto the building adjacent to the inn; the lurching rotary movement of the turret shook the building debris from the tank like a wet dog drying itself. There were a series of clunks echoing from within the tank; the gunner was loading a shell into the barrel breach. The shouts between the driver and the gunner could just about be heard over the idling engine, having its own exchange of explosions and hot metal. A short, sharp howl of an order preceded the striking of the firing cap triggering the detonation which could almost be heard; the shell, as wide as a clenched fist, accelerated, twisting with finesse as it followed the rifled length of the barrel, until finally the light at the end of the bore was met, and the projectile could head on its way to deliver the payload of explosives.

Another blast, and once more, aged construction materials were scattered through the dense atmosphere, knocking a handful of Germans to the hard ground, two or three of whom were not to rise again. This time the unfortunate building was not levelled; the roof was cleanly removed, leaving what remained of the charred boards of the first floor to protect the level below from the elements. There was, however, sufficient room for the mighty gun to be manoeuvred and aimed at the inn.

One of the younger members of the allied squad retrieved from his inventory a sticky grenade, and hurled if from his post on the first floor down to the tank; it stuck to the thick armour plating just above the caterpillar tracks on the left side of the tank. He threw a second for good measure, with a smug victorious grin on his supple and youthful face; this time the gooey surround of the high explosive clung to the side of the turret like a barnacle on the bottom of the boat.

"Fire in the hole!" chanted the inexperienced soldier, ducking below the base of the window frame.

As intuitively as retreating from a hot object, all of the rest of the group immediately took cover upon hearing the phrase; an automatic reaction bred into them. In quick succession, two short, solid thuds shook the ground, shaking yet more settled dust from the beams above, drifting like snow, gently onto the scored floor.

The young soldier yelled a cheer high to rafters as he emerged from his cover to see that the tank had been unaffected by the explosions; the thick armour plating was sufficient to resist incoming tank shells, so it simply shrugged off the pitiful attempt to be breached with the inferior explosives. The arrogant smile of the recruit quickly receded and turned into an expression of confusion and worry; like a rabbit in the headlights, he stood petrified in his window, a cold sweat running down the contours of his spine. The other soldiers silently scorned at the incompetence and lack of knowledge this young fool showed, some loathing his presence in their battalion.

The bearings within the fully operational Panther turret groaned as the barrel was repositioned towards the centre on the inn. The German forces took cover, crouching behind the tank or within one of the few surrounding buildings that had complete frontal brick-work.

"Everyone out the back! Move, move, move!" The orders were barked by Cpt Briggs.

There was a crooked stable door, already ajar, adjacent to the fire place at the back of the building. The group leader bounded to the middle of the room in a flash and began gesturing, waving his arms trying to hasten the exit and get all his men out alive. Without question all the soldiers turned about and made headway for the heavy door, desperate to step over the threshold between survival and death. The two men up on the first floor leapt down in a controlled panic, hitting the ground heavy, both men crumbling at the knees, outstretched weather-beaten hands grazing along the splintered wooden boards. Dragged to their feet by the nearby allied fighters, all the men sprinted out the back door, followed by Cpt Briggs.

The heavy oak door led out into a small back alley with a cobbled surface, surprisingly clean and free from debris. Enclosing the path were low pine fence panels painted a simple light brown, most of which were in one piece, undamaged by the terror that had been raining down on the broken city. Over the fence panels were what would once have been neat gardens, leading down from the terraced houses which stretched either side of the inn, and now containing wild grass long neglected but still green and lush; there were greenhouses, a dull grey in colour, housing no life, with large shards of broken panes lying on the cold, mud trodden slabs; vegetable patches had long since been devoured by any passing wildlife, taking whatever they could in the heat of this animalistic war. The majority of the buildings that still stood looked rather respectable from the rear, and almost inviting and homely. The roof lines were drooped towards the middle; the aged slate, thick with lichen, painted a calm white and yellow sea across the rooftops.

The tank loosed a shell into the inn; there was an explosion of cement and wood splinters. Like swarms of sharpened stakes, they flew arrow-like towards the small battalion. All the troops had hit the floor with the sound of the explosion, covering their heads. The remains of the inn came to settle on the cold, coloured cobbled stone work, clunking and ringing with musical patterns which were hypnotic, and nearly kept the soldiers glued to the floor, wanting to hear more of the subtle harmonious tones. Almost reluctantly, the men rose to their feet and continued their escape; all except one somewhat inexperienced soldier.

The whole group stopped as the young soldier howled in agony, still lying on his front and trying to get himself up, trying to keep going, trying to stay alive. Westfield was closest to him, and rushed over, conscious that the German forces would be bursting through the rubble heap of the unrecognisable inn at any moment; he hurriedly rolled over the young recruit onto his back to reveal a large portion of a splintered oak beam protruding through the man's stomach. The recruit was breathing rapidly and deeply, in an irregular fashion, and reached into his top jacket pocket with a trembling hand to pull out a small plastic vile of liquid, resembling a small tube of toothpaste; it was a syrette, morphine and syringe all in one, issued to every soldier. He looked up at Westfield, his bottom jaw quivering, and gestured for the liquid to be administered. Westfield gingerly took the vile between thumb and two fingers, rolled up the soldier's sleeve and pieced his upper arm. Westfield squeezed the syrette to force the liquid into the draining veins. The recruit chocked slightly on the warm red drink filling his mouth, ejecting a fine spray which stained his lips. He swallowed hard and nodded repeatedly, with an indefinite movement that suggested he was drawing on strength he didn't really have.

"I can make it. I can make it!"

The young soldier sounded so certain, had such hope in his soft voice that Westfield truly wanted to believe him. The cold stone cobbles were being glazed with a warm crimson. His strained his head free from the ground and grabbed the log sticking through his abdomen with conviction; with both hands he tried to remove the object, crying out as splintered fragments were pushed deeper into the soft tissue. He had to stop, and looked to Westfield with teary eyes which screamed 'help' so loud it was painful.

"I don't want to die!" He forced out his simple words to Westfield through gritted teeth.

Westfield's vision was starting to blur as his eyes became watery, knowing that there was nothing he could do to save the young soldier, young enough to be his own son. The recruit threw his hands to the reddened floor and attempted to clamber to his feet. Grunting in agony through a grimacing face, he got to his knees, at which point he had to stop once more. Looking at the floor he noticed the river of blood meandering between the stones; he closed his eyes as tears hydrated the ground and gently sobbed while shaking his head.

A shot was fired and the recruit collapsed face first, down into the small gullies running with dark rivers. The shot was a clean entry through the back of his head, a merciful execution. Westfield staggered to his feet in a hurry, only to be frozen stiff, mid-stance, by the sight that he beheld: Briggs was standing tall and dominant over the collapsed body, the muzzle of his Webley pistol smoking ever so slightly.

"He was done for. If we didn't do it the Germans would have done much worse"

He spoke in such a manner so as to reassure *himself* what he had just done was justified and merciful. Everyone was shocked by what had just happened. Contrary to how the young soldier pleaded, there was no hope for him; at least this is what they all hoped was the case given what had just happened. The group leader tossed the young recruit onto his back, collected his ammunition and supplies and ripped away his dog tags: Jimmy Hill, that was the boy's name, and nobody even knew; he had been seen as the over-confident new kid, showing off and trying to impress the other men; the fool who would go and get himself killed.

Cpt Briggs ordered the men onward, to survive. Without a second thought or glance, they all continued to run down the alleyway, praying that they would find some form of salvation at the end.

THREE

The allied soldiers thudded, heavy footed, over the slippery, uneven cobbles with considerable pace, despite each carrying half their weight in supplies and equipment on their backs. The quality of the fencing was gradually deteriorating the further they travelled down the inclined escape route. The rotting panels encasing the path came to a dog-leg in the otherwise arrow-straight route. In single file, they darted through the chicane section, breaking their line of sight back to the dismantled inn; if the enemy did emerge through the wreckage, then at least they would not be able to see where the they had fled to, thought the soldiers in unison.

Cpt Briggs was leading the race, when suddenly he stopped, raising a hand, signalling for his followers to do the same. Obediently they all came to a halt, somewhat confused and anxious that they were no longer escaping from certain death. There was now the clear sound of German forces making their way over the destroyed inn and charging down the alley; the inn was about a thirty second run from the group's current stationary position, the sounds being carried on the light gritty breeze.

Silently, Cpt Briggs ordered the men over the fence, into an adjacent garden and to lie down, right up against the barricade and not to make the slightest sound. Westfield was one of the last to leapfrog the spongy, rotten fencing. He ran down the fence line to the next available space where he could lie down, tucked up cosily to the moist laths and directly behind a fellow comrade. He lay still, face down in the prickly grass with his eyes closed so as to enhance his hearing: the clear rhythmic sprinting of the enemy forces accompanied by Germanic shouts was growing louder and trembling the ground more and more, so much so it seemed like the degrading fence, the group's first line of defence, was going to wither like wet cardboard. A lone bird sang nearby, darting through the crisp, crunching leaves of deceased shrubbery, scratching at the dry earth in a desperate search for rations. In the distance there was the faint burble of aircraft up in the now wondrously cyan sky, free from the steely grasp of the cloud cover that had been lurking, and the sun shone with a brilliant intensity, painting a fresh pallet of colours across the scene; the grass radiated with a luminescent forest green, the slab stone path down the middle of the garden sparkled and glinted diamond-like, leading down to a small shed at the bottom of the garden which had faded lime green paint blistering and dropping onto rich dark chocolate soil of a desecrated vegetable patch, and what remained of any glass in the small shattered windows reflected rainbows onto the fencing, which was given a fresh coat of compost brown, somehow highlighting the defects and fragility further.

The enemy had reached the dog-leg along the cobbled stretch and had slowed their pace to a brisk walk: the path was a long straight after that section, and they were clearly suspicious of the fact that they could not see the group running on down the path; they knew that a game of hide and seek was underway.

The enemy force was far too large and strong for the allies to stage an ambush; all they could do was hold their breath and whisper to the heavens for some good fortune. Westfield shot open his eyes when he heard rustling from right in front of him; the soldier lying down ahead was fighting to hold back tears of both fear and rage. Westfield had a face-full of trembling black boot soles, deep grooved and well caked with mud and dust.

The German forces were walking directly by the groups sanctuary, with a definitively slowed pace which implied they were becoming increasingly quizzical and alert. The rustling soldier was going to end up getting them all killed, thought Westfield; to him the noises were amplified, like somebody was beating the dust out of an old rug with a large oar, while someone else was kicking their way through a forest of dried leaves and dead twigs.

Westfield felt the need to try and control the man, since the quivering soldier was now a thinning line between survival and suicide. He sharply took hold of one of the soldiers rustling legs in an attempt to suppress the noise produced. The man yelped in a panic and yanked at the trigger of his rifle, the muzzle of which had been butted up against the boot sole of the soldier ahead; the thick rubber offered no resistance to supersonic lead.

Their position had been compromised. The enemy immediately started to riddle the rotting fence panels with bullets; the soft wood flew apart and careened across the narrow stretch of garden, and there was a firework-like explosive mist of red, which permanently pinned some of the soldiers to the ground, painting a crimson abstract pattern onto the emerald grassy canvas. The leg that had been quivering was doing so no more, although Westfield was still holding onto the limb, his mouth dropped and eyes wide in horror as it dawned on him what he had just unleashed by trying to attenuate his comrades error; his heart actually slowed whilst his face turned as pale as the moon and he swallowed hard, all the time simply starring at the back of the leg which had caused all the trouble.

Cpt Briggs and three remaining men were crawling alongside the fence line, galloping on all-fours like small antelope up towards the back of the house the garden belonged to, hoping they had not been seen and could make the seemingly lengthy journey to the back of the derelict terrace. The enemy troops were still all in the alley, firing into the fast disintegrating fence. The popping of all the various rifles and machine guns produced a tone that gave a swooping sensation and went in and out of phase with itself, resulting in a hypnotic white noise.

A single bullet streamed through the hand of Westfield that still had not released the leg of his dead comrade. He was blown out of his self-pitying trance and threw himself backwards to land facing up to the delightful clear sky. As he had been lying at the back of the group, furthest down the fence, he had escaped very nearly all the gunfire. There was no hope of him being able to join Cpt Briggs and the other three, but this didn't even cross his mind as he began to scramble on all fours, like an overexcited mutt on a polished floor, to reach the back of the shed at the bottom of the garden. He sat upright, with his back to the shed, which blocked line of sight between him and the Germans, and nursed his hand, pulling a bundle of grubby, torn bandages from his equipment bag and quickly spooling it around his wounded trigger hand in a desperate attempt to stop the bleeding; the bullet had shot between his index and middle fingers towards the edge of the hand, passing clean through with the only trace being a dark solid ring, leaving him unable to articulate his middle finger.

His heavy adrenaline fuelled breathing made him somewhat lightheaded, and the sight of the already bloodied bandage induced a nauseating sensation deep at the base of his tightened chest cavity. He was facing the opposite row of terraced houses, those which the path would have led to; they seemed his most likely form of salvation. There was no way he would be able to hop the fences from garden to garden to move parallel to the rows of houses, he would undoubtedly be seen in this open backyard playground and shot dead; and that would be if he was lucky. He couldn't just sit there and wait for everything to blow over either, since he wasn't in the best of hiding spots, sitting by a shed in the middle of a garden about to be searched by a horde of adrenaline and hatred pumped enemy troops. His hand had started to throb excessively, as though his heart had relocated to his right palm, causing his fingers to involuntarily twitch with each rapid beat.

His mind worked overtime, processing all the possible routes and all of them being calculated to have the same probable, undesired, outcome. Starting to panic, his heart beat faster still, forcing semi-congealed blood through the fine web mesh of the bandage, which he saw from the peripheral of his vision just drip onto a couple of stray house bricks at the corner of the shed.

After an overly quick thought process, he leant across to take one of the bricks with his left hand and hurled it over the fencing to his left, over the cobbled alley to crash down in one of the surrounding gardens; being right-handed, the brick clipped the far fence and broke into two red, crumbly parts and just clambered over into the garden behind the German forces, who were starting to enter the plot Westfield was currently hiding in.

The plan failed; only about a dozen or so Germans went to investigate the new noise, only to find nothing. Westfield was trapped; no means of escape and nothing to make a last stand with, having abandoned his weapon in an undignified panic. He reached into his breast pocket of the tattered uniform, and pulled from it a single bullet; it was no ordinary round, but had a hollow tip, for maximum effectiveness. He hurried through the contents of his rucksack to find the revolver, which had all six chambers empty. He had no time to think before loading the lone bullet into the gun, readying the firing hammer. Closing his watery eyes, he hurried the gun into his dry mouth, and with the run of a single tear down his cheek, yanked at the trigger…

FOUR

It was the pitch of the night, black as tar, as the light aircraft bobbled over the clouds, fluffy and slivery in the partial light of the half-moon. They hadn't intended on the moon showing its face; it greatly increased the chances of getting spotted. The soft dim glow of the blood red light in the back of the small aircraft hid the fear on the young face of Corporal Bill Myers, while the drone of the two small engines and wind rush past the thin fuselage drowned out his racing heart. It was his first in-action parachute drop, coupled with the fact he would be jumping into the inky blackness with his life-saving parachute likely to glow like a beacon from the moon. He sat on one side of the plane with his back to the small round windows, his legs shaking in unison with one another and his moist palms in a prayer arrangement; he had never been a churchgoing man, although he was promising to do so if he made it down to the hostile ground in the same physical state he left the plane.

Across from Myers sat his superior, Captain Finn, looking calm and collected, as he always did: he was sat in a relaxed position, with his feet spread, arms gently folded and head thrown back with his eyes closed. He had been in this situation a number of times before, and had received his share of broken limbs and scarred tissue to prove the fact. For each drop made, he had tattooed a simple tally line up the inside of his right arm. He also had ink up the inside of his left arm, crossed out swastikas, one for each and every kill; it was easy for him to count each kill, as he was a sniper. He remembered the faces of every man he starred down the scope at before pulling the trigger, and not for one instant did he feel the slightest hint of remorse.

The cargo netting along the inner sides of the plane clinked and rattled, and boxes on the floor slid this way and that, never settling, making short shushes as they traversed the icy aluminium floor; it was difficult to properly focus on anything or determine true colours due to the softly burning bulbs bathing everything red. The pilot and co-pilot would occasionally say something to one another, which was only ever essential flight information and nothing more, delivered in quiet and strict tones.

"Approaching drop zone" the information was delivered by the co-pilot in a confident voice, crisp and clear over the noises of the burbling propellers, rustling consignments and turbulent air.

Myers sprang to his feet and immediately got into a tangle trying to put on his parachute over the top of his rucksack. Cpt Finn rose majestically and calmly began to collect his items and get ready for yet another jump, having almost the look of boredom upon his strong, square-cut face. Within moments he was prepared, and stepped over to Myers to help the poor man, like a fish caught in netting.

"Come on soldier, pull it together. It's going to be a long time down there if you act like this. And it's *not* going to be a long time before we lose our heads if you keep acting like this" Cpt Finn delivered the words to Myers in a cool, fatherly tone, trying to calm the nervous boy; there was no need barking at the whimpering soldier to keep calm, as that would only make things worse. Cpt Finn was a man of few words, but knew just what to say, when and how. He helped Myers with his equipment, like dressing a youngster for a first day school, and read off a mental checklist, all the time speaking on the same level as the Cpl and allowing the inexperienced recruit to feel as though he could take charge of the situation.

"Drop's coming up. Stand-by. Wait for green" another perfectly clear and concise message was relayed from the front of the plane. The two men made their way down the narrow body of the aircraft to the exit hatch. On their fronts were their precious single chutes, cared for like a mother with a newly born baby; there was no reserve parachute in question. Bolted firmly to each of their backs was a rucksack, half their size and loaded with more supplies than could ever be needed, plus the most important ingredient for this recipe to succeed, the Lee Enfield rifle, cleaned and serviced to perfection, and fitted with a high magnification scope, each and every lens of which hand polished to the highest quality. The rifles had been placed delicately into the bags with the butt of the rifle protruding from the top of the rucksack.

"This is the one. We stay focussed, we stay alive" Cpt Finn gave a firm grip on Myers' shoulder as he delivered another short and inspirational speech in his deep, gravelly voice.

Cpt Finn stepped back a pace or two, ensuring he was behind the line marked across the floor, and Myers quickly imitated the action precisely, before checking and re-checking a number of times that his parachute was welded to his chest as tightly as it could be, so much so he left himself unable to take a deep breath as the rear hatch of the plane slowly opened up, like the mouth of a whale; a resonant hum and whine sounded through the plane. The hum then yielded to the urgent rush of air past the hatch, much more intense and at a deafening volume. The cargo netting wafted and beat even more violently against the thin sides of the plane, and the weight of the contents in the boxes on the cabin floor was all that prevented the thin splintery wooden structures from hurtling down and out the back.

A lone bulb to the left of Cpt Finn suddenly burned a bright green, reminiscent of a freshly mown lush meadow in the height of spring. Cpt Finn made his short run up and leapt from the aircraft, falling with the style and grace of an eagle hunting its prey. After a few attempted deep breaths, Myers followed suit, and left the noisy drone of the aircraft only to drop into a deafening pounding of white noise. They hurtled towards the mass of black and brown, with the dim and temperamental half-moon light occasionally giving them glimpses of dark spindly trees, silvery dry stone walls and an inky river.

They fell towards the ground in a spread eagle position; Myers had been told this was the easiest way to control the fall, not that he felt the slightest bit in control, but more as riding passenger on a derailing train. The wind roared past the cold ears of Cpl Myers, and his hair waved in an accelerated fashion. He squinted his glistening eyes which streamed as trickles of high velocity atmosphere breached their way past the threshold of his poorly fitted goggles. He desperately fought not to close his eyes for fear he would not deploy his parachute in time, even though the two men were simply relying on their ability to count backwards from a given number in a regular sequence, predetermined by a group of number-crunchers they had never met or even heard of; when they hit zero, the rip cord was pulled.

The sudden deceleration from opening the black circular parachute jerked the men upwards like they were tethered to the plane, the slack of which has just run out. Gently they began to drift to the barren land, now no longer forced to endure the torturous wind rush, but able to take in the sights and sounds of the landscape: there were distant flashes over the horizon which illuminated the fractured cloud cover like warning beacons, followed a number of seconds later by low thunderous rumbles; the sky seemed to change to a more inviting shade of deep sea blue between the intense flashes, and allowed the brightest burning stars to bring attention to themselves, exploding silently millions of miles away against a backdrop as black as the fast approaching ground. The soft drone of the light aircraft could not really be heard, and what sound did prevail was soon terminated by the overly-long low pitch growls reverberating from the pounding shells over the terrifyingly close horizon, which was only released from the grip of the darkness with each successive flash. The light-show resembled the sapphire, silver and lavender of an electrical spark, discharging like lightning, giving a panoramic display around the entire night sky. The land appeared mostly featureless, not helped by the inability to see great distances between the illuminating flashes, which were actually welcome to help guide the men to the ground; historic stone walls encapsulated the scraggly fields, which themselves were like woven mats drenched with iced mud. Aside from the artificial thunder, the only other sound was the rustle of nearby bushes, or possibly some nocturnal creatures scurrying, oblivious to the dangers and bloodshed.

Gentle tugs on the appropriate lines allowed Cpt Finn to weave and steer into a clearing in a darkened field which he had somehow spied long ago through the thick murky ether; vigorous and frantic wrestling with the chute from Myers led him straight towards a lone tree, standing as a strong silhouette against the flickering horizon.

Like a duck to water, Cpt Finn swooped in and with a swift short jog, brought himself to a neat stop on the marshy terrain, allowing the billowed parachute to float and nestle into the ground before he turned to check on the progress of Myers, whom he never once smirked or rolled his wise eyes at. He scanned the area to find the young corporal desperately trying to dislodge his parachute from the dark canopy of a spindly tree.

Shadowy silhouettes leapt from the depths of the icy darkness as they were backlit by the distant catastrophic light display. Cpt Finn hurriedly folded and packed into his rucksack the deflated chute before squelching across the land and dodging the tufts of grass to reach the bruised corporal; he could just see through the murky night that Myers' parachute and rigging were caught up in the tree, and that his feet were not firmly planted on the unstable marshland. He pulled a large knife from his waist, which stole any available light in order to shine softly against the gloomy backdrop, and although his eyes could not fully adjust to the vision impairing blackness with the incessant distant light displays, like camera flashes in a gloomy prison cell, he proceeded to free the trapped corporal; feeling his way over the coarse textured bark, of what was probably an old oak he thought, he sensed the repetitive, spiralling contours of the parachute cording, and immediately hacked away. He continued the ritual, probing across the abrasive bark, through the twiggy branches, between the soft leaves and finally reaching the taught line.

Cpl Myers eventually dropped the short distance down to the wet ground, landing on all fours, soaking the arms and knees of his tweed uniform. He quickly rose to his feet to assist with the removal of his torn parachute from the unharmed tree; they couldn't leave any trace of their arrival.

Stuffing the useless chute past his rifle and deep into his rucksack, Myers pleaded his case to Cpt Finn.

"I don't know what happened, I couldn't see the tree, it was so dark, and the flashes put me off and..."

"We're down in one piece. Enough, or it'll cloud your judgment" the stern tone stopped Myers in his disjointed stride, who nodded shamefully.

"Now tell me, what is our primary objective?"

"Eliminate the sniper threat…"

FIVE

The revolver held in Westfield's sweaty grip banged with a light click; he opened his eyes which were pulsating with adrenaline and ready to pop from his skull. Removing the gun from his quivering mouth in an instant he set about investigating the problem, looking all-round the item with a confused glance about his face, dripping with a cold sweat; he had loaded the bullet into the wrong chamber, a simple mistake to make, but not one to make twice.

With his stiff left hand, well weathered with a coarse leather-like look and feel, speckled with pinpoints of dirt and the odd blade of stray grass, gently he clicked the dull grey revolving cylinder twice, so that the golden casing of the lone bullet shone through a slight gap at the back of the cylinder. This time the round was definitely in the right place: with a pull of the trigger, the cylinder would revolve, smooth and reliable as clockwork and with a reminiscent tick; the firing hammer would strike the centre of the blasting cap at the back of the casing, igniting the gunpowder to send the hollow lump of lead down the rifled barrel.

Once more he reluctantly offered up the gun and found himself starring down the mesmerizing pattern of the rifled barrel. He breathed deeply, almost sighing each time; he forced a stiff upper lip, although his bloodshot teary eyes coupled with his gritted teeth painted a truer picture. He pressed the cannon hard into his temple and dreamt of home: his wife whom he had known since he was seven and knew he had wanted to make her so happy since he was seven and a half; his five year old daughter, making him daisy chains and swinging in his arms in the back garden of the family home. All those things he loved so much, and here he was making the decision to never be able to see them ever again. Through a grimacing face he broke into tears, sobbing quietly enough so as not to draw attention. Tears as pure as a mountain spring rolled over his cheeks, raining down onto his dirty, worn uniform trousers.

A single shot was fired; a heavy thud signalled a man dropping to the ground.

***

Once again Westfield sprang open his weary eyes and pointed the revolver anywhere but at himself. A second and a third shot sounded, echoing off the surrounding houses and creating a reverberating background noise, as the Germans all fell to the floor to take cover, producing an uninterrupted rush of shuffling and banging, not knowing where the shots were being fired from. There was the unmistakable pop of allied rifle fire, followed by the lubricated sliding of the bolt action, chambering another round with a tick and a tock, in a rhythmic fashion, and there was definitely more than just one rifle being wielded, maybe three or four, all cracking one after the other. From behind the shed Westfield listened with intent to the symphony taking place, and thanked the heavens for the intervention that allowed him to make an immediate decision to tumble clumsily over the rickety fence ahead of him and run up to the back of the house atop the long garden. He had left behind all his equipment and the sten gun, although his cramped hand had not permitted him to release his iron grip on the revolver. Not even making the time to wipe his face, he found himself scrambling, almost on all fours, with blurred vision, seeing only a lush green sea with a bleary dark mass ahead; no further detail was permitted via his tired, streaming eyes.

Reaching the back of the house, he threw the heavy patio door along its steel track to the side, sending the glazed frame crashing into the buffers at the end of the rail, only then to shudder back towards its starting position. Westfield all but dived into the desolate sanctuary, the sitting room showcasing a sorry looking scene: there was a low, long coffee table of a colour akin to roasted beans, which was surrounded along its length by two sofas; they were grey cloth with some sort of faded pattern on them, although they had small tears, revealing the yellow sponge underneath like bright sunlight shining through cracks in a wall. There was a small opening in the end wall where a fire would have once crackled and spat hot ash to create the small dark marks in the what would once have been a soft cream carpet, now dirt trodden and dust laden so as to appear a patchwork rug of distress. The walls looked as though they were sighing, the wallpaper peeling away towards the top to produce a claustrophobia-inducing arc around the top half of the room; the wall underneath the softly striped light lime green paper was almost a vibrant pale orange, the plaster crumbling away like the face of an eroding sea front.

Closing the door promptly he was able to take stock of what was going on in the opposite garden. It was Cpt Briggs and his band of three warriors making a stand against the enemy force from inside one of the houses, two doors up from the garden where all hell had broken loose, and where the Germans now took refuge. Westfield watched intently, but with care so as not to give himself up; he remained away from the dirt splattered patio window, within the shadows of his sanctuary. The house was on higher ground than the opposite terraces, allowing Westfield to see clearly that the four allied soldiers were on the top floor, standing back from the small, dark window frames, which contained only glass remnants around the inside edges.

Having spied the muzzle flashes, the enemy forces ran towards to the house occupied by the allies, staying low and weaving, trying to avoid the incoming gunfire. A number of soldiers were hit, spreading their colleagues with a thin burgundy splattering as they fell to the floor, some yelling for help which never came as all the other soldiers were set on not receiving the same fate, and eliminating the allied threat. One of the maimed soldiers started to crawl towards the back entrance of a house, trying to remove himself from the sights of the allied gunners; he stained the lively green grass with a dark shade of red, groaning with agony as the friction pulled at his stomach wound. He slumped to smeared ground as a whistling bullet exited the side of his head with a crack, resembling the yolk spilling from an opened egg.

Gazing down the length of the garden, Westfield looked on as the soldiers went in and out of view, passing behind the shed where he had previously taken refuge, hopping over the splintering fence line to pass behind a row of low tress, obscuring all but the heads of the soldiers foolish enough not to stay low. The Germans reached the back of the house after scrambling in an untidy manner over another chestnut brown fence. The ratio of the two opposing forces was staggering, and still the allied group rained down with everything they had, not giving up. Although they had barricaded themselves in, the enemy's might had soon splintered the already heavily damaged door, and they rushed up the stairs.

Westfield watched, helpless, as the vast enemy force disappeared from the trampled garden into the house like water draining through a sluice gate. He could almost hear them thundering up the soft carpeted stairs and throwing open the softwood door to the cosy bedroom, furnished with pinks, yellows, and now lavished with reds. There was a firework display in the small room, with bullets driven by hatred whipping across and through anything in sight. One of the four men, already visibly wounded, jumped from the window; whether an attempt to save or to take his own life, he hit the concrete path with a solid whack and did not move again, his neck at an acute angle to his spine. Not satisfied, the enemy force that had yet to enter the small house turned and riddled the corpse until there was little to be recognised as a man's body.

A great cheer erupted from the small room in the small house, so loud it was painful for Westfield to listen to. He didn't want to continue looking, but was frozen stiff in a stance with one foot forward, fists clenched by his side and teeth gritted hard; he could see the German forces up on the first floor, looting any belongings of his poor allied comrades; although the goings on at the bottom half of the room were out of view, he could see the German's swinging their legs sadistically, and knew just what that meant was happening to his fallen team; his throat jolted as he gulped hard, turning away while biting his lower lip, hard enough to leave an impression. He slowly sank and sat back against the wall opposite to the patio window on the coarse glass scattered and thread bare carpet, and dropped his pounding head into his bloodied, stinging and tired hands, the soft and moist bandage being the only comfort that was to be had. He gave a gentle sob. Feeling alone and confused as to what to do, he simply sat and sat, staring vacantly at a picture abandoned on a wall; it was of a boat on the open sea, painted in a somewhat abstract manner with no definition to the features. In the fast dimming light he could make out the green sea and possibly a brown wooden hull; the glass in front of the picture had a small spider web crack from the top left corner, and the gold painted wooden surround was flaking and splintered; nothing more could be clearly seen, especially since Westfield was really only looking at the picture in his peripheral vision as he became lost in the middle distance. Struggling to his feet, he made his way out of the saddening room via a door into the hallway, and subsequently traipsed up to the top floor of the abandoned house, so as not to be spied by ground level patrols; there were prolonged creaks as he ascended the bare pinewood staircase, grasping the banister as he went. At the top of the flight, he made a rather unusually slow and reserved scan of the settings, twisting his head this way and that. He shuffled on into a small bedroom to the right and closed the lightly coloured door behind him gently. There was a look of desperation and shear sorrow upon his face. He sat once again with his back to a hard and uncomfortable wall, opposite the half-height bedroom window and then resumed his despairing tears while watching the slowly setting radiant sun sink behind the wavy roof tiles of the opposite buildings; the reddening light bounced from tile to tile giving a kaleidoscope of patterns to behold. From his angle, Westfield could just see the absent roof line which was where the inn stood not so long ago.

Not knowing if he wanted to wake up, he tucked up against a corner and removed his heavy, stained and pungent jacket to pull over himself. He closed his eyes and tried to, at least temporarily, escape the thoughts of the forthcoming inevitabilities.

SIX

Cpt Finn and Myers had located a disused barn during the night where they managed to get some sort of rest. The building was not of sound construction, with the thick wood beams rotting away and being home to a multitude of insects. The twin doors did sit square within the dark oak frame and were permanently ajar, permitting a draft to enter and disturb the piles of sodden, decomposing hay, which attracted further swarms of insects to the pungent aroma that diffused throughout the barn. The hard compacted soil that was the floor was mostly strewn with moist hay and straw of an unhealthy brown colour. The two men had with them sleeping bags which they had deployed on an upper level of the barn, keeping them out of sight of any persons that may have wandered in. The upper level had an area roughly a third of that of the ground area, situated along one side of the building and gave a gallery vista of the expanse of barn below. Six upright beams ran the length of the barn supporting the upper level; each of the solid, square sections had been blackened with years of excessive muck and debris. Judging from the appalling state of the rest of the structure, it was questionable whether the beams would support the weight of the two men and all their gear, but without too much deliberation, Cpt Finn had made the decision to venture up the steep steps; the soft planks did not so much creak as squelch as he ascended to the sleeping quarters. There was a thin covering of straw, brittle and prickly from the length of time it had been sat there drying, over the suspect bowed and warped boarding. Cpt Finn checked the upper structure with a simple stomping of his heel, kicking up dust and causing the straw to bounce as though on a trampoline. After little computation, he cast out his long green sleeping bag like a cloth being flung across a table; he signalled Myers to do the same with a long nod of his head, who had been obediently waiting at the base of the ladder, looking upward expectantly. There were small eddies of dust that could just be seen through the gloom, rising up and quickly dying away again on the barn floor as the freezing air pushed through the riddled exterior.

Myers climbed into his sack and rolled onto his side, ensuring his face could not be seen by his superior. The corporal brought his hands to his face and let out a number of deep sighs, his sorely tired eyes shut tight against the black night.

The early morning sun streamed between the gaps in the exterior lath work and through the array of holes riddled all over the structure, creating a complex puzzle-like pattern on the windswept, mucky floor, which danced across the space with a fluid motion and changed colour from a deep cherry to a vibrant orange as the morning progressed.

Myers opened his dreary eyes, which were bombarded by the intense inferno forcing him to clamp them shut for a minute or two more. When he could eventually look around, he found that Cpt Finn was already packing away his sleeping bag from the less than restful night; aching limbs and a freezing howling wind had contributed to his lack of sleep.

"We need to make headway for our post. The earlier we get there, the sooner we can make sure we know exactly where this guy could be hiding" Cpt Finn spoke with a fully alert tone, but had a slight hint of worry to his voice. "We're already running behind".

Myers wriggled from his sleeping bag and with heavy eyes he stuffed it clumsily into his rucksack, giving sharp shakes of his head to prevent himself from drifting off and stalling Cpt Finn further.

They quickly marched on in silence and in single file with the sun almost directly ahead of them, forcing the men to squint fiercely to keep the intense rays at bay. Frequent compass checks from Cpt Finn signalled to Myers they were on the right path, and the sun gradually yielded, moving off from the direct sight line to their upper right, scorching the bruised arm of Myers through his damp uniform. The radiant sun sitting in the blue sky dotted with feathery silver clouds gave a luminescence to the knee high yellow crop and the bluey-grey stone walls framing the picturesque rolling fields, which were assembled into a patchwork of greens, yellows and browns. They were marching through the crop at the edge of the fields so as to reduce the chance of their obvious tracks of flattened crop being spotted by passing enemy and potentially compromising the mission. They rubbed shoulders with the stone walls segregating the fields, the uneven knife-like flints dotted along the structures snagging their sleeves, the wild brambles tugging at their angles.

Cpt Finn ceased his assertive forward motion through the natural obstacles and slowly made his way to the floor, making sure his body was covered by the low crop. Myers copied the captain's movements precisely, taking off his rucksack and snaking into the crop to better camouflage himself, fluffing up any bent stalks in his immediate surround so that there was no clear depression in the field to any onlookers.

There was a road up ahead, cutting between this field and the next. Cpt Finn had spied movement: it was a small German battalion passing, their laughter and humming heard over the rustling crop and chirping birds. He removed his rifle from the rucksack lying adjacent to him and starred through the telescopic sights, getting a crisp and clear view of the enemy force with a few adjusting *clicks* of the scope lenses. There were thirty or so men, and a troop transport truck; it was probable the soldiers had all piled out of the lorry to enjoy a walk alongside the picture perfect fields on a gorgeous day, untouched by conflict, but there were no certainties. Cpt Finn could easily have pulled the trigger, and it is likely the men would be non-the-wiser to the whereabouts of the stray sniper, but it wasn't worth the risk, there were far too many foreign guns. He was not one for taking unnecessary risks, and always one for completing the task he had set out to. He let the day remain gorgeous and untouched by conflict.

There was nothing to do but lie and wait in the baking heat wearing heavy, itchy clothing while lying in claustrophobic, tickling crop that attracted insects, making the air thick with aphids, impairing breathing and almost inducing a cough, a luxury that could not be taken for fear it could be the last. A quarter of an hour came and left, and after a second quarter hour of boredom and discomfort had arrived and passed through, Cpt Finn slowly rose from the nauseatingly irritable hiding spot, checking to the distant left and right, before finally fully escaping from the solitary confinement of the field. Myers immediately leapt from the ground and brushed himself down, removing all insects and plant debris, which he had been playing with and crushing to try and pass the impossibly uncomfortable wait. Regathering their things, they headed onward, rifles now in hand with the knowledge that enemy patrols operated in the vicinity. Keeping to the edge of field after field, they made their inefficient journey to finally reach the outskirts of Berlin as the sun ducked below the contrasting horizon.

They made their way around the scars in the battered land; deep craters randomly placed amid the picture postcard, richly coloured terrain, and yet it did not look out of place when in the background stood the decrepit ruins of former civilisation, the brickwork and rubble of family homes still warm. People had been driven from their homes, and now had little to return to, but this did not keep the men from walking on to find shelter in the first building they came to which had not been levelled in a hurried detonation of falling explosives. In a subsided house that could be referred to as anything but homely, they spent the night, up on the first floor, sleeping in shifts while the other guarded the rickety staircase. Feeling pretty sure no-one would emerge up onto the darkening, blast damaged landing, Myers dozed off, leant up against the door frame of their small room which was offering sanctuary for the warm evening.

The small room had once clearly belonged to a young boy, the walls painted a vibrant blue which was peeling away from the cracked plaster, and there was a thin band of wallpaper which ran around the middle of the room, depicting Volkswagen Beetles in assorted colours, torn and losing adhesion to the wall. The carpet was a soft blue, pocked with scorch marks from falling ash. A toy chest sat in one of the corners, full to the brim with trains, action figures, toy guns. The wooden chest was labelled on the front with scrawly, infantile writing, stencilled on in thick black marker pen; *Christof* was the boy's name, and Cpt Finn's mind ran away with him, unable to wonder anything else but whether or not the child got out of the building alive. It troubled him deeply, chilling him from his fingertips, clutching his rifle for security, all the way down to his toes, blistered and enveloped by damp socks from the hard days walk. Tightly curled in the corner, he forced his beaten eyes to stay shut, and tried to drift off into a surreal dream world, where the words 'war', 'innocent' and 'child' had never been uttered in the same context.

The morning sun flooded into the heart wrenchingly empty bedroom, and having long been awake, Cpt Finn vacantly starred on at a shaft of scattered light passing through the broken window glass, highlighting every speck of dust dancing randomly through the room before they finally reached the coarse ridges in the carpet to join the dull rainbow that had been cast.

Hearing German voices close by, Cpt Finn quickly checked his rifle, which he hadn't loosened his grip of all through his distressed night. He moved towards the window with definite but quiet actions, keeping his back to the wall and staying crouched down, his head remaining below the line of the window sill. He slowly turned around and raised his squatted position ever so slightly, just bringing his eyes over the top of the ledge, allowing him see down into the street below. There was a group of four enemy soldiers, all huddled in close to one another, making what Cpt Finn assumed to be idle conversation and sharing a single cigarette as they walked up the sun-beaten muddy street, dirtying their already grubby black boots and frayed trouser legs. Each of them was wielding an immaculately gleaming MP40 sub-machine gun, held waist high in bruised hands dotted with cuts and blotched with dirt. Their steps quickened and they galloped towards a house on the opposite side of the long curving street, a few houses along from Cpt Finn and Myers. They charged through the front door, reducing it to little more than kindling. There was the slamming of doors, short sharp shouts and an underlying hum of heavy boot fall over the springy floor boards; they were searching the houses, checking the area for allied soldiers. The Germans emerged from the house seemingly seconds after entering, and resumed their casual walk. One of the German's had held the cigarette, half burned, loosely in his lips as they searched the house, and after a quick puff he proceeded to share around the small, comforting artefact. After taking a moments breather, they charged on the next house.

This unexpected threat had to be dealt with. Cpt Finn quickly snapped off the protective lens caps on the telescopic sights and made comfortable his grip on the Lee Enfield; after a snappy glance down the sights he expertly adjusted the magnification and focus, setting it perfectly for the range required in the blink of a sleepy eye. He remained somewhat concealed, not wanting the enemy to see him before he had seen them off. Subsequent to emerging from the house, the Germans continued their strange pattern of relaxing a little before storming the following house; this time they turned to face the side of the street where Cpt Finn and Myers were, and continued their cycle on a house about four or five doors down. Although the street curved in such a way that he was able to just see the house being searched, he would not be able to get off a clear shot. Not being one for anything but perfection, he patiently bided his time. During the Germans current raid, there were additions to the pallet of sounds that had not been heard previously; shots were fired. Cpt Finn jumped at the unexpected pops, which echoed off each house and carried up the length of the street; his eyes widened with shock, and then squinted with hatred.

The four soldiers emerged, bearing smug smirks on their rotten faces, Cpt Finn though; still he waited. Everything had to be just so for this to go his way. Again, the enemy group attacked a house, adjacent to the previous; they seemed to be clearing two at a time on each side of the street, which meant that after this house, an opportunity would arise. Cpt Finn could not quite see them emerge, although he heard them, and glared down his sights and through the crosshairs, waiting for them to emerge from the left of his deadly tunnel vision. The first German emerged, but Cpt Finn did not take the shot; he waited for all men to come into view while making their way across the uneven cobbles to their next house of call. Cpt Finn was resting the barrel on the window ledge and had the heavy wood stock pressed hard into his shoulder; he knew it was more than just bad practice to not stand back from a window, for danger of the rifle being spotted, but he had assessed the situation and deemed the increased accuracy he would achieve to be of greater priority. With his left eye closed hard, he glared through the spotless lens at the magnified images, precisely lining up the crosshairs over two men, one standing behind the other; he calmly pulled the trigger.

He didn't have time to watch as the bullet screamed through the chest of the first man before coming to a halt in the waist of the second; both fell to the floor, the man with the abdominal wound was still alive, and had a somewhat puzzled look of agony on his face as he yelled in the quiet street. Cpt Finn instantly operated the bolt action slide, expelling the spent brass cartridge and slotting a fresh round into the breach; all the time he kept a fixed stare down the sights. He made the second shot; a reverberating shudder sounded around the neighbouring brickwork and the recoil kicked him back slightly in his crouched position and dislodged his light hair from its ruffled form. The bullet sailed through the neck of the third German, dropping him to the floor, dead before the blood had stopped contaminating the filthy streets. The fourth man ran into the nearest house and took cover behind the front window, crouching low, and out of sight. Once more Cpt Finn smoothly operated the slide, which made a comforting clicking, the rhythm having an air of clockwork about it. He could not pick out the fourth man, and so turned his attention back to the second German, who was crawling across the ground towards the safety of the house, still unknowing of the whereabouts of the shots. Cpt Finn positioned the thin black lines over the magnified ear of the man, and holding his breath he slowly squeezed the trigger.

Another slick reload and he began searching the poorly lit room of the opposite house for the final German, slowly sweeping across all aspects of the house and taking an extra moment to look at any slight movement or anything remotely suspicious looking. The remains of torn, scorched curtains gently swayed as a cool breeze casually drifted in and out of the house, a shadowy sofa sat still in the middle of the room, any colours or features concealed under the eerily silent shade.

Myers had only just awoke, and did so with a start, as Cpt Finn just began his search for the final kill. The corporal was lying up against the doorframe to the room, which was coarse and in places down had been stripped of its white gloss down to bare softwood. He hastily rubbed his eyes in confusion before grasping his rifle which had been cast to his side and onto the landing; there was a look of guilt on his face and a degree of upset in his eyes, which had yet to adjust to the radiant sunshine, forcing him to squint slightly. Unsure how best to act, he sat with his knees up and back against one edge of the door frame so that he was neither in nor out of the room, and loosely held his gun in a cradling type fashion; he looked on with a solemn expression towards the back of Cpt Finn, feeling helpless.

"You're awake then? Sorry I woke you" Cpt Finn poorly joked in his gravely yet comforting tone, with not the slightest hint of sarcasm or anger.

"There's a final guy who's just being a little… awkward. Could do with a hand here" Cpt Finn once again proved he always knew exactly what to say as Myers' ears pricked up and he almost shot to his feet with joy.

"Yes! How can I help? Anything!" the young corporal stuttered his words in excitement; it was his chance to show his worth to this father-like figure of his.

"Right. Listen…" the captain quietly conveyed his message, all the time looking down the scope of his rifle, "…I know he is in the front room of the house over there. I can see both exits for the room so he can't have escaped. I have got two rounds left before I need to reload, which I'll fire off. Making a less than subtle reload, I'm hoping he will pop up to take a shot at me while I can't shoot back. That's where you come in…". Myers listened with intend as though he was a six year old being told his favourite bed-time story; a slight grin across his face and beaming eyes as Cpt Finn continued. "You'll need to be at the ready, and you'll take the shot. Clear?" Cpt Finn remained starring down the sights as he quizzed the young corporal on his attentiveness.

"Understood, sir!" Myers replied in a brash tone as he clutched his rifle and began to make his way out of the bedroom.

"I'll make the shot from the downstairs front window?" He tried to speak with a confident and assertive manner, but he phrased the words as a question, and it was clear from his slightly cracking voice that he was fishing for approval.

"Very good. Sixty seconds 'till I fire. Count both shots"

Bounding down the stairs, Myers made his way urgently to the front room, and stood back from the window, just as he had been taught to do. He took a moment to check the magnification and focus on his sights, but could not quite get them absolutely spot on in the time allotted by Cpt Finn. He consulted his clunky matte grey watch; almost show time.

The first shot resounded: Cpt Finn had aimed just above the rotting window sill of the house, below which he believed the soldier was hiding, trying to make it seem to the German that he had been spotted. The shrapnel from the shattered round tore a hole in the carpet and blew stuffing from the sofa, creating a thin haze of luminously pristine white feathers. From the room below, Myers heard the smooth reload of Cpt Finn, the clunk of the empty casing as it hit the floor and rang out with a faint high pitch note. The second shot was fired, triggering Myers to look through his sights with the utmost concentration. Cpt Finn had aimed the second shot at the wooden cabinet towards the back of the room, hoping to instil into the German that the person shooting at him was of temperamental aim. The bullet shattered one of the dark wood doors and scattered the pieces across the once cosy room, piercing the upholstery feathers which were still drifting lazily to the worn carpeted ground. Cpt Finn began to make his obvious and timely reload, holding his rifle up to the window while crouching down to allow the noise to transmit as loudly as possible; he forced back the bolt action slide with aggression and removed the spent magazine, tossing it against the far wall of the small room, the thin metal tingling like small bells as it struck the partly crumbled plaster. Rummaging through his organized uniform pocket he found a fresh magazine brimmed with bullets, and with a slow motion like haste attempted to slot it into the base of the weapon, intentionally missing and striking the sturdy wooden stock of the rifle, which gave a soft glockenspiel thud.

A shot was fired. Then a second shot banged, almost too soon after the first, Cpt Finn thought, puzzled.

Hearing the echoing ripple of the fired round had signalled Cpt Finn to slot the magazine precisely into the rifle and scope the situation: he dropped the box of bullets, which he watched fall to the floor almost in slow motion with a bemused gaze upon his face. He felt the small shock up through his aching and cramped legs as they hit the floor, only to spring back up ankle high before coming to rest on the carpet, revealing a ragged puncture mark in the magazine; the thin black metal had torn and twisted and now protruded out, like the damage from a pen punched through a piece of card. A glance at his tense and throbbing left hand dropped a large piece into the puzzle; one of the shots had not been taken by the corporal.

"I got him! I think I got him captain!" the ecstatic young corporal shouted from below, shaking his clenched white knuckled fist in the dusty air and almost jumping up through the ceiling with pride to see the look on Cpt Finn's proudly beaming face.

"Good lad" Cpt Finn spoke softly under his breath, his eyes fixated on the small patch of carpet he could see by looking through his hand; blood readily flowed from the wound, situated below his thumb, and of more than ample size to fit his little finger through. The viscous crimson fluid added to the stains and trodden-in dirt of the blue carpet. He was sat heavily on the floor, slouched forward, the buttons on his prickly green jacket straining. Knowing exactly which of the small pockets on the front left of his rucksack to check, he retrieved small pieces of pristine white gauze along with a brown glass bottle. He moistened the gauze with the anti-septic liquid and placed a single segment each side of the wound, wincing as he did, and followed it up by encasing the majority of his hand in a continuous band of snowy white ribbon.

"Did you see? Did you see captain? I shot and he fell back, so I think I got him" Myers was leaping up the flight of groaning stairs, almost stomping through the hollow steps with joy.

"I was worried I saw him shoot right before I did but I guess it was the sun reflecting" Myers was still speaking in a very rapid, excited manner as he jumped up onto the landing and raced into the room; there he found Cpt Finn with his back to the opposite wall sitting under the windowsill, gently holding his left wrist above his heart in an attempt to slow the bleeding and suppress the throbbing. Myers stopped in his tracks, stunned by the sight he beheld; he felt as though he had just shot his own father, albeit an accident, but not easing the guilt to any degree.

"I don't... know what to say... I'm *so* sorry" Myers spoke slowly with a lump in his throat, struggling to string together his apologetic words.

"I wanted to make sure I got him, for *you*. I took my time and that's why I... I mean I should've... I did get him though in the end... I think... I..." He spluttered through teary eyes, not looking directly at Cpt Finn, his blurred vision scattering the shapes around the room, unable to focus on any particular details; he bit his quivering lip when he paused, allowing himself to regain some composure.

"Get down lad" Cpt Finn spoke assertively but not with aggression, gesturing with both his hands: he had looked up from his wound to notice the sun illuminating Myers from the neck down, and had ordered the corporal to move out of sight of the window, *just in case*, he thought to himself.

"It's fine, don't panic. It's barely even a flesh wound. Now, what we need to do is to confirm the kill, correct?" Cpt Finn had once again phrased the question in such a way as to make the corporal feel as though he was in control and making decisions for himself.

"Yes, yes we do... but I err... I really am sorry, sir" still there was the look of remorse upon the corporal's face, as he crouched down below the line of the window.

Myers moved across the room in a squatted position to help the captain to his feet, and they both gathered all their items then made their way, crouching, across to the stairs, and permitted themselves to stand tall for navigating the crooked, creaking steps. Cautiously, Cpt Finn made his way out of the front door, with his rifle being held strong in just his right hand, while his left hand was tucked into an inside jacket pocket close to his chest; he was closely followed by the obedient corporal, and together they quickly walked over to the opposite house, and glanced in through the shattered front window. There they saw the German soldier lying at the base of the window in an almost circular pool of his own blood; he was still alive, breathing very rapidly and had his hands clenched around the legs of a bulky low coffee table, which lay just up from him, towards the edge of the room, and he was attempting to haul himself up onto his feet, or even his knees, but he simply did not have the strength left in him.

"He's your kill" Cpt Finn nodded towards the German victim with a vacant countenance. In a fluid motion he turned away as Myers pulled a pistol from his waist. There was frantic German speak as the soldier saw the pistol lifted and pointed towards him; somehow he had mustered the energy to make frantic hand gestures and signals before showing a blood stained photograph he had been holding in his hand of his wife and two son: Myers chose to not comprehend the signs.

SEVEN

It was still morning, and the two men continued onward with the warm sunshine on their face, following the desolate rubble strewn streets towards the inner outskirts of Berlin. Cpt Finn was leading the way, his rifle slung over his right shoulder, like a manual labourer carrying a heavy shovel; his injured hand prevented him from holding the gun in a proper manner.

"I just want to say, I'm sorry again, captain" Myers had been itching to utter the words for some time.

"These things happen in war. I'm still in one piece, well nearly one piece!" Cpt Finn gave a little chuckle, trying to put a light hearted spin on the matter. "I'll hear nothing more of it now, and I don't want you thinking any more of it. It will cloud your judgement and leave you unfocussed" his tone switched from jovial to deeper and more serious.

A squall of silence went barrelling round the streets, drowning out the crunch of debris underfoot and the pops of distant gunfire.

"So, have you got anyone special waiting back home for you then?" Cpt Finn's tone changed again, sounding much more relaxed and his gravelly voice much silkier; he wanted to break the tension and give the corporal something else to think about.

Myers took the bait and began an autonomous ramble about life back home. Cpt Finn shut most of it out, just hearing muffled murmurings as he proceeded to navigate, checking the alignment of the sun with the hands of his watch and adjusting their direction of travel accordingly through the increasingly derelict streets. Black and white houses edged the street like piano keys and the sun was getting higher in the sky, beating down hard. The sight of missing houses along an otherwise continuous row was becoming more common, as was the feel of more uneven and potholed roads, and there was a stench of petroleum and gunpowder becoming increasingly intense in the acrid air.

It seemed a long time walking to Cpt Finn, shown in his tired looking, dirty face, his wrinkles darker than the surrounding skin from all the trapped grime, exacerbating his age. The intense heat from the sun had been raining down on the two men all afternoon, reflecting off the whites of the house frontages, the browns and greys of the dusty, worn roads and the slivery mirror-like puddles which were dotted along the way. Initially the breaks between the series of houses revealed lush green overgrown grasslands with some golden corn-like reeds escaping the chocking clutch of the neglected scrub, but with each parting of the black and white fronted terraces, the backdrop became increasingly urban, although mostly with crumbling shells of former buildings. It was more and more apparent to Cpt Finn that with each step, they were heading further into unknown territory, and were beyond rescue, should anything go wrong: they were on their own, with no exceptions.

They continued to follow the snaking road, the dust and rubble pattern of which resembled the scales of a lightly coloured reptile, until their destination came into view over the artificial horizon created by the crooked, slate grey roof line of the houses: a tower block, which was scarred from surrounding impacts, but somehow still standing. The aged grey of the concrete absorbed most of the hope giving light, and the holes where windows had once been resembled the dark sunken eyes of a slimy killer, and delivered a spine twitching evil stare.

"That's it" Cpt Finn broke the silence which had been persisting and spoke softly under the wind, "That's where he is" he was referring to the objective: an enemy sniper was camping in the tower block and removing allied soldiers from miles around and giving early warning of air force movements. Cpt Finn knew there was more to the overall problem than just a decent enemy shooter, but he also knew that eliminating the source would be a fast and effective, if only temporary, solution to the menacing problem.

"We will need to keep cover from now on, can't have him spotting us, can we" Cpt Finn spoke his rhetorical question in that way he did so as to make Myers partly feel included and important.

"We stay focussed, we stay patient." Cpt Finn paused, awaiting Myers to finish his instructional motto.

"…We stay alive…" Myers finished.

They moved off the streets and started walking behind the long curving row of houses, which allowed them to remain out of view of the tower block, with some occasional crouching as a result of wilted buildings that otherwise gave cover. They pushed onward, their objective now in reach.

EIGHT

Westfield was relinquished of a tiring and restless sleep when the early morning sun scorched the side of his face, baked with blood and dirt. He had been lying in a small, emptied room, bare from any home life or warmth; the wooden floorboards felt as cold as steel, the tattered walls and sloping ceiling were as claustrophobic as a prison cell. He sat upright with a start, taking stock of where he was, quickly darting his not yet adjusted eyes around the blindingly bright room.

He had nothing with him. He had left it at the bottom of the garden of the opposite house. He had no hope of surviving if he had no equipment, and it wasn't the *offensive tools* he had in mind, but provisions and water, and something to try and prevent his still throbbing hand from turning gangrenous. He looked down at the loosely wound bandage, thick with clotted blood and heavily mired. He got to his aching feet and collected his jacket, swung it round and slowly put it on; his injured hand prevented him moving any faster. He shuffled his way to the top of the stairs and made his way down, like he was walking in his own home to start a lazy breakfast. The bare steps groaned as he plodded down, and he had not a care for the noise he was making. He made his way to the back of the house, to the picture window, which still framed the desolate remains of the inn and bodies strewn across the land. The sun was behind the house where Westfield was standing, casting long, morning shadows down the length of the garden, highlighting his footsteps from the previous night in the long grass, more a bile yellow than a lush green in the sunlight.

Without even first surveying the area for enemy patrols, he forced back the patio window with his left hand, leaning into the movement and using his mass to move the sticking steel framed door. He stepped heavy footed down onto the once lightly coloured stone patio, now thick with grime and growing a green weed in the shallow puddles. He stopped for a moment, just to sigh, before continuing his fearless plodding to the bottom of the garden, almost staggering across the width of the untended lawn like a sleepy Sunday morning stroll to the bathroom. As he reached the fence at the bottom of the garden, he did not slow, but walked almost straight over the top of the low, light brown fence, tumbling over the decaying wood to land hard on the concrete ground where he had sat just a day earlier, pistol in-hand loaded with just one bullet. He sat for a moment on the cold, hard ground, his bloodied hand still up in the air and clutching the top of the splintered fence. He commenced a moronic laughter as he retrieved his hand from the ragged fence; the bandage had become caught on the wooden barbs, unravelling it from his hand chaotically like cotton unwinding from a reel dropped to the floor. He stared at his right hand, at the loose remains of dirty bandage that trailed up to the fence, at the barely coagulated wound, the accruing red stain in the fabric. He swung his right shoulder like he was hurling a discus in order to dislodge the thin piece of bandage atop the fence line, and his head wobbled loosely as he did so, his vision of the shed ahead of him would have been blurred if he hadn't had his eyes half closed in a sleep like trance. He clawed at the bandages in a frustrated and clumsy manner in an attempt to dislodge them from his hand; he caught the partly congealed wound, tearing the scab from his palm and pulling at the fresh skin surrounding the hole, ripping small rivers of red which ran towards the edge of the swollen, purple hand, tender and raw all over, yet he did not give the slightest flinch. He discarded the spent dressing with an over arm bowl at the shadow of himself swaying across the horizontal laths of the copper-brown shed. The lightweight cotton moved in an accelerated drift and struck the shed wall, where they caught on the rough wood, partly dressing the shadow figure in a royal blend of red and white robes. He slowly lowered himself to lie to one side, his head pushed hard into the corner of his left arm, his rigid elbow pressed against the ageing concrete, glistening with all colours of aggregate. He let out an unconstrained cry in his baggy green sleeve, the fibres from which made his face itchy, but he could not do anything other than cry. His mouth was open and saliva dripped in its viscous way onto the ruffled uniform, changing the colour to more of a deep sea green than a lush meadow. There weren't many tears, although enough to contribute to the inner elbow of his jacket becoming warm and clammy as he mopped his face in rapid movements. The shadow figure had melted away, giving Westfield the privacy to sob on the ground alone; his breathing was erratic, and his back juddered with each respiration. He had unknowingly shifted himself into a less awkward spread on the floor, subconsciously knowing he would be there for more than just a moment.

He awoke, having fallen asleep face down, on the surprisingly inviting sparkling concrete. The sun was climbing up through the sky, but mostly blocked by wispy clouds, restraining the intense rays to just give a post-apocalyptic throb of dull light from up in the leaden sky. His eyes stung every time he blinked, which he did so in a laborious and heavy manner. Dragging himself in an almost helpless way over to the shed, the tweed of his uniform rustled as it snagged on the rough terrain and his metal buckle grated. Reuniting himself with the abandoned rucksack, he wasted little time in searching for food rations; he tore open a foil packet and greedily poured the dehydrated contents straight from the silver bag into his dry mouth. He chomped away vigorously, making the sound of a piglet crunching walnuts. He discarded the glinting packet over his shoulder and hastily retrieved the matte aluminium flask, and poured the crystal liquid from the decanter; the water splashed across his face and dripped out the corners of his mouth giving at least part of his face a much overdue rinse, carving clean lines in the speckled dirt. Once satisfied, his stomach sloshing with liquid, he slowly screwed the top back onto the decanter, which gave a light squeak as he did so. He stuffed the much less heavy metal can back into the rucksack and wiped his mouth with his left sleeve, utilising the corner at the elbow that was already moistened, rubbing dry his face in short head movements.

It had only just begun to register that his hand was painful, although it had looked sore and possibly infected for some time. Westfield rummaged around the inner of the sack and pulled out his syrette; he toyed with the idea for a little time before tossing it back into the pack. Next he found some ointment from a side pocket, and gingerly applied it to the just about clotting wound; even if the application would only numb the pain by means of a placebo effect, he would be content.

He grasped the rucksack with his aching left hand and made his way to blistered feet; he put on the rucksack like a heavy raincoat, and pulled the dusty black tabs tight, anchoring the receptacle to his back. His weighted eyes, beaten with grit and swollen with anguish, caught the glare of the revolver out of the peripheral of his vision; it glinted temptingly. A quick snapping open of the chamber revealed that the lone bullet was still just that, and an equally snappy *click* to reassemble the hand-canon left it poised to function. He held it quite gingerly, and had a look of almost guilt upon his face; he glanced around, crouching down a little, spying for any onlookers, and not because he was afraid of being shot by the enemy, but in case anybody were to witness the strange emotion upon his face.

In a swift movement he removed the sack and placed the gun in its own compartment on the side; laboriously, he tucked it away as though handling an explosive. The sun was gaining height in the clearing sky, the shadow man, who had reappeared, was shrinking away into himself.

Strolling over the dry, crisp grass, similar underfoot to that on a frosty morning, he exited the garden via the fallen fence panel and stepped into the alley, cobbled with rainbows of stones. He made his way to the left, up through the dog-leg walkway and towards the back of the demolished inn. His face somehow looked less tired, the lines across his brow seemed fewer and farther between, the creases around his mouth were not as deep. His dark, wispy hair was still ruffled, but in such a way it looked like an indulgent lie-in was the cause, and his stubble darkened the underside of his head like it was intentional. An individual was lying across the path up ahead of Westfield, and he quickened his pace slightly, although he did not break into a run.

The man was almost unrecognisable, what with his abused form; the neglected fence line had been decorated with an abstract effect. The sun retreated behind a steel-wool-like cloud and the area was bathed in a cooling faint light. With his bottom jaw clamped shut and the corners of his mouth downturned, he stared on, disguising placing his hand to his mouth as a clumsy stroke of his stubble ridden face. He glanced round, attempting to take stock of the situation. He turned about on his worn heels and marched franticly down the narrow path, travelling away from the inn; the dilapidated soles caused him to skid backwards on the glassy cobbles, forcing him to catch his balance. He made a double-take so lively that it blended into just a single glance back;

nothing was registered, not even the corpse on the ground ravaged and being left to decay within the rotting ruins of the acrid city.

Skidding out onto what looked like a quiet housing street, he veered right, with no justification behind the decision, and walked quickly, sticking close to the black and white fronted terrace houses edging the long sweeping road.

Blood was swelling from his pulsating hand, which he held across his chest tightly with his opposite hand. As he all but ran through the quiet streets, he could feel the congealing ooze clutch at the weave of his jacket like the fingers of ivy on brickwork; occasionally he forced back his hand to break the semi-solid bridge between flesh and tweed, a light sound like the soft tear of Velcro accompanied the clatter of his shoes to fill the empty air. As he continued to hurriedly walk onward, to somewhere, he kept his hand routine in time with his disjointed march strides.

Drunk on over exertion, he persevered forward, almost stumbling, catching his footing occasionally as he followed the winding cobbled road, increasingly strewn with rubble from felled buildings, the air thick with mortar dust which tickled the throat.

***

Westfield came to the edge of a clearing, although it hadn't always been. There was a square slab of grey ahead of him, edged with stumps of red brick perforating the ground, and decorated towards the middle with yet more loose masonry, accompanied by broken glass and shattered dark wood. There was a road which ran along each edge of the large square, disguised by the buildings and houses which had crumbled at the knees to fall face first and lie helplessly across the streets. To his right he was amazed to behold a towering structure, of much greater height than the remaining standing buildings dotted along the perimeter of the square. He looked the structure up and down, having to shield his eyes from the sun which was not quite covered by the back edge of the tower.

A shot was fired.

He did not feel the warm metal though. Or hear the icy crack of a ricochet. The screaming lonely silence was broken, and with it came on a spell of self-preserving agoraphobia; desperate for sanctuary, he scrambled into the tower through a roughly barricaded entrance.

NINE

After a back aching crouched walk, Cpt Finn and Cpl Myers came to some sort of clearing around the base of the tower block. They were still at the rear of the buildings, although they stood taller than previous structures they had passed, possibly four or five stories high, allowing the two men to stand and walk comfortably in the war zone without being spied. The tower stood at one corner of what looked like a square, which was piled with cracked bricks, bent ironwork and shards of glass, making up molehills of debris around the area. The captain and corporal came up behind buildings which stood on the adjacent corner from the tower block; to their left was the second tallest building around the square. On the far corner, opposite, the buildings did not so much stand as lie in a helpless, crippled heap, thrown out across the space.

Cpt Finn's fist sailed up into the air, strong, like a lighthouse in a storm, against gusts being funnelled by the enclosing structures. He crouched down; Myers immediately followed and glanced around with nervously dancing eyes, straining to search the surroundings which were cast in a meagre light. It felt like the sun made a complete circuit of the leaden sky before Cpt Finn spoke with a light whisper.

"This is it. We'll set up watch in this building here, see?" He pointed through the light-strangled alley at the reddish brick structure that they could access without having to go out into the road. Myers made no noise, but nodded with understanding to show attention. As he did so Cpt Finn continued.

"We'll set up watch over night" he repeated softly, "sleep in shifts and keep an eye out. Give it a while, observe what the happenings are. Can't go home empty handed after all this, but by the same token, impatience and sloppiness won't win us the day either" he began to lose the whisper and his voice became firmer, "stay focussed, stay patient, and stay alive!".

"Right, let's move." Cpt Finn walked stealthily, swiftly followed by Myers.

The line of buildings curled around to the right, giving more than sufficient cover from the prying black-hole eyes of the tower block. They came upon a ground floor window with light auburn boards nailed from the inside, though fortunately loose enough to be pried apart and give a sufficiently sized aperture to allow an undignified scramble into the building. The windowsill was cast concrete and littered with small stones, spherical and motionless like the dew on early morning grass. Having handed his equipment to Myers in an attempt to reduce the noise he would make, Cpt Finn entered first, sliding through on his front, holding his stomach muscles tight to prevent the wind being squeezed from him like bellows. He shimmied and weaved and lowered himself, like a snake trying to remain concealed, onto the concrete jungle floor supporting a myriad of pea sized rubble particles. Bussing all the equipment over to Cpt Finn like a waiter at a service hatch, Myers hauled himself up onto the ledge with a little jump and proceeded to drag himself across the aggregate occupying the window ledge, rustling up a sound of dried autumnal leaves being crushed by weather-beaten hands.

Having dragged the corporal through the window and subsequently pulled him to his feet from the dust laden floor, Cpt Finn set about barricading the window, gathering short wooden planks and positioning them over the already half-blocked opening. He expertly placed them, secure enough to stay in place with a stiff wind, he thought. All other ground level openings seemed secure, and so they made their way up the naked concrete steps to the higher levels. By keeping to the back of the building, the risk of being spied from the tower block was slim, as the shooter would be up towards the top levels, Cpt Finn knew. The danger would increase significantly by venturing near the windows at the front of the building, no longer boarded as they ascended above the ground floor.

They trudged up the stairs, making a soft scratching noise with the contact between the thick soles of their boots and the loose pebbles. A gust from the thick, bitty atmosphere forced Cpt Finn to halt abruptly while partway up the final staircase. The roof was absent from the building, giving a panoramic view of the surrounding destruction; burgundy brick building fronts, a darkening teal sky being shut out by an encircling iron curtain of clouds, yellow mortar dust drifting in the air like feathery ash and settling on the coarse and jagged structures, the ominous tower block, somehow maintaining the same level of eerie leaden glow even with the retreating sun.

"Back, back!" Cpt Finn whispered to Myers, who was following close behind. He did not look back, but gestured with low, waving hand signals to the corporal as he ducked his head to ensure cover from the towering block of concrete straight ahead over the castellated brickwork. Myers pivoted clumsily on his heels and bounded down the solid stairway and skidded out onto the floor below. Promptly he went over to a supporting pillar, briskly walking with a hunched stance. He stood with his back against the column, clutching the rifle in his scarlet hands, throbbing with adrenaline. Stepping backwards down the pale grey staircase, Cpt Finn soon emerged from the blindingly dull light falling down through the roofless gap at the top of the stairs, highlighting a column of ashen dust speckles contrasting against the light starved floor space. Upon landing his foot hard on the solid flooring he shot around and charged towards Myers, bursting through the shaft of floating dust, disturbing the random drifting of the insignificant specs which glinted with a shimmering light like that of a dying star. With a sense of urgency, Cpt Finn charged straight past the corporal and went to a column nearer to the unglazed windows to gain a view of the tower block ahead.

He squatted with his back against the pillar, facing away from the windows, and dropped his head, his eyes closed; he made a sigh that Myers thought was heavy enough to disturb the thick, detritus covered floor. Peering round his column, Myers starred at the captain, his eyes darting all over his body: his dark hair was dirtied with a fine, chalk like dust and sat irregularly upon his head; the uniform, ruffled and soiled was stretched taught across his knees and his hands loosely held the rifle across his horizontal thighs, his one hand an angry purple in colour. Myers silently swallowed hard and looked anywhere else for a moment as he became overwhelmed with guilt, his heart rattled against his ribs in xylophonic fashion and his warming face invited beads of sweat to run down into greasy eyebrows.

"We'll camp here. Stay on the lookout. With a bit of luck he'll give something away, slip up" Cpt Finn delivered the softly spoken instructions clearly, although there was a strange element of hesitation and uncertainty that echoed around the harsh stone room during his pauses.

Forcing himself into the pillar, sliding his back up the coarse concrete with a soft sound of snagging wool, Cpt Finn rose slowly to full stance. After a sharp stretch he made a deep, heavy squat, resembling a man retired of his chores, and plonked his rucksack on the floor next to him, puffing a cloud of ashen masonry dust into the already hazy and contaminated air. He had initially positioned himself so that he was supporting his weight with bent legs, but he soon yielded and allowed the roughly poured concrete floor to offer some comforting support, dropping with a solid, muffled thud.

"Captain?" a look of puzzlement came upon the corporal's weary face as he proceeded to ask, in a sheepish manner, what he did not want to hear the answer to. "Captain, are you ok? Is everything alright? Can I help?" his tone became more exacerbated as he continued with his inquisition. His eyes widened, mouth gaped and his ears strained in the direction of the slumped captain.

"No" he said simply in an uncharacteristically blunt response.

"Err..." Myers' breathing became pronounced, his chest straining to shift the weight imparted by the rucksack straps.

"I... Urm..." the corporal continued his painfully stuttered groans of perplexity at the sight he beheld. His dark, furry eyebrows crinkled down over the top of his pale azure eyes which caught the late afternoon light to glisten like a setting sun over a receding tide. He shook his head ever so slightly, his mouth open and becoming dry to the point he thought his face might crack. With ferocity he blinked his eyes, and his voice became strangulated and thin.

"Please sir." He felt as though he had been gargling nettles and inhaling brambles.

"Please!" he crouched involuntarily, placing the Lee Enfield rifle on the cooling stone floor, and scrubbed the greasy wire-like mat of hair at the back of his head in a nervous fashion.

"Tell me what to do!" he barked, with disregard for the echoing walls.

"Keep your... voice down... lad!" Cpt Finn spoke in a sullen tone during a succession of exhales, recuperating energy during the short pauses to allow him to breathe in again.

"Don't give... the game up now" the captain's uniform was an irregular shade of patchy camouflage green and his face a cotton white; crystal beads were falling from his needle-like stubble, splitting the last of the dying light into brilliant rainbows as it shot through each teary drop.

Myers was standing again, holding the butt end of his rifle, the muzzle buried into the dusty concrete. He was breathing heavier and more erratically than the captain, his chest juddering, eyes wide and cheeks moving like bellows as the cold air whistled through his tight mouth.

"WHAT SHALL I DO?!" he leaned in on the aching balls of his feet to howl the order towards the slumped captain, who did not even flinch at the distressed bellow from the corporal. Myers' outburst had sprayed a fine mist of saliva through the tense air, glistening like spray from a waterfall, which hit the ground and soaked up a local area of dust, producing a dark blotted circle of damp that spread with an almost infectious quality, contaminating the light floor.

Myers gave a deep inhalation, forcing his lungs hard into his rib cage, stretching out his chest.

"ANSWER ME!!!" the anguish laden cry ricocheted between the concrete pillars, creating a silence so still it was painful to endure.

The corporal was breathing in a deep, rhythmic fashion through flared nostrils, forcing dank and tepid air over his stiff lip, raised just slightly to bare gritted teeth. Myers approached the captain and knelt, placed a hand on his shoulder and looked to him like a frightened child to their omniscient parent.

"You look awful my boy" Cpt Finn had conjured the energy for a few words, and had selected them just so to try and ease the mood, trying to slay the unwanted attention of the present matter.

A more than simply awkward silence lingered in the stale air; Myers was looking down from his knelt stance at Cpt Finn who in turn looked down at the leaden floor. Myers could not see Cpt Finn's eyes, which he was glad of, for he knew that they would be heavy, longing for sleep. They both shifted slightly in an uneasy and unsynchronised manner.

The absolute silence was softly shattered with a start.

"Are you going to die...?" Myers spoke hesitantly but very seriously, looking at Cpt Finn directly at the top of the captain's head, who was staring down. "...Because of me?" he continued, like a reluctant child in a guilt ridden tone.

Cpt Finn raised his head and looked vaguely into the concrete cell; the cold and colourless room, baron but for the stocky pillars erupting up through the floor, the light somehow stifled despite the regular windows along the clinically bare walls...

Blood surged through the veins of Cpt Finn and his inky black pupils dilated sharply, allowing all the colourlessness of the room to flood in and be processed; his haphazard and slow blinking ceased as his eyelids seemed to recede permanently deep beneath the grease ridden, wiry eyebrows. With an almost slow motion air about his movements, he somehow pivoted about his waist to face the oddly aged face of Myers. Like grappling hooks, he threw out his arms towards the corporal at his left, digging into the tweed uniform, and with a throw of his weight to the right, the captain dragged the corporal down, who, like a felled tree, hit the solid floor hard. There was a slight displacement of coarse grained dust which briefly masked the face of Myers, before settling to reveal a patchwork of detritus across his ignorant face.

"You fool!" Cpt Finn barked in a hoarse whisper, looking deep into the innocent eyes of Myers.

"Have you not learnt anything? Can you not get anything right?!" the characteristic rhetorical questioning had a much different tone about it than was usually the case.

"You're going to get us killed!"

Cpt Finn gritted his teeth from under his tensed mouth and shook his head with sheer disapproval, glaring into the middle distance as he did so. Myers still had a look of bemusement upon his face. His eyes glistened wildly in the starved light and his contrastingly arid mouth was dropped just slightly. He felt his heart race and breathing hasten as the captain continued to gesture with his head movements.

Cpt Finn gave a reverberating gulp and shut his eyes tiredly; a small tributary ran hastily from the corner of an eye to the acute corner of his mouth.

Both men remained still and remained quiet as awkward silence graced the room and took up residence for what felt like hours; wispy eddy currents swirled grey dust across the floor with the clatter of dry rice strewn over flag stone tiles. The mid afternoon sun broke free from encaging steel cloud and beamed a shaft of light down the steps which seemed to ascend to the heavens.

Cpt Finn's throat made a slow succession of movements, like a steeplejack up and down his ladder. He then burst open the thick silence with a lugubrious tone to his voice.

"I had a son" he began solemnly, like the start to a grave novel, "*had* a son" he iterated, still looking away from Myers, "he was seven..." he paused, trying to disguise his sorrowful breathing as a vacant sigh.

Myers was looking on intently, still with a look of guilt upon his immature face.

"We were on holiday on the south coast" Cpt Finn continued "small cottage in a remote village overlooking a spit of land." Another pause and a gulp with a tilt back of his head.

"The perfect place" he continued dramatically, but not over exaggerating his buried emotions "we were walking along the coast, the lad holding his mother's hand ahead of me. The path was loose stone with spindly bush roots scattered on one side, and a grassy embankment on the other, decorated with all the colours of wild flowers before stopping to reveal the pure blue of the sea. You couldn't see the rocks, but you could hear the surf breaking" the story seemed to have reduced his booming gravelly voice to a velvet whisper, albeit slightly choked and stuttered.

The strangled light split through the crystal film glazing the captain's eyes, and with a quick tense of his bottom jaw he went on with a crackling sorrow to his voice.

"He tripped. I saw him trip over the log, laid across the path. I didn't do anything, it was too quick. His grasp broke free from his mother's hand and he staggered, tripping over the path edge. He went bounding down the bank, flowers tearing and flying up as he went, flailing. He was gone even before I was running down the bank. I crawled to the cliff edge and peered over but saw nothing; he was gone. To this day I wish I had jumped in, there and then, if only to find his body" he gave a deep sigh and rubbed his stubble with his infected hand "I should have gone in."

"And you know what the worst part is?" the rhetorical question was not in the context that Myers was accustomed to, "I remember the screams, the cries, the yells of fear, knowing full well I couldn't do anything. I remember that all too clear. And yet I can't –" his voice started to break just slightly and he gave a rapid wipe of his eyes, "I can't even remember his face. My own sons face!" he gave an anguished shout. "That is worse than this hell hole! That is true torture!"

"I'm sorry to hear that sir, but it's not –" Cpt Finn cut Myers short, and continued as though the Corporal had never been speaking.

"Straight away I was angry. Angry at *her*. She was still on the path and I shouted up to her, shouted *at* her, I suppose would be more accurate. I blamed her for letting go of him. Said that she should have gone over before he did. She was crying, but I didn't believe it. I scrambled up the hill, full of hatred and grabbed her delicate shoulders, and shouted in her face. She screwed up her face and shut her eyes, and I kept on, kept… just kept screaming at her" he looked down to the leaden floor heavy heartedly, clearly not wanting to continue the sorrowful tale.

With a short, sharp sniff, and through a lump in his throat, he ashamedly said "I shoved her, just cast her away like I was throwing a wet towel to the sandy coloured stones on the ground, and she fell flat on her back. The look of absolute terror she gave me; that, I regrettably *can't* forget. Her beautiful eyes, so watery that they shimmered, and her furrowed brow and delicate cheeks taught with that expression. It haunts me."

There was a pause.

Myers recognised that there was more to come, and remained quiet. He had adjusted himself so that he was leaning against the pillar directly to the right of Cpt Finn.

"I didn't hit her; I would like to think it's because I'm better than that, but I know that's not true; she was simply out or reach. So I kicked the path stones at her. The air became a thick yellow with the dust. I spoke with a..." a brief pause as he collected his thoughts, selecting the right words, "*calmer* tone after that, I didn't yell anymore, but the undertone was worse, like I was really twisting a knife in her, like I was wishing death upon her. *I can't even look at you* I simply spoke through gritted teeth"

Still Cpt Finn gazed straight ahead into the room, not bearing to even glance over at Myers, who was looking upon him, still with hope and belief in his eyes.

"Don't really know what happened then; she was going the same way as the boy. It was like a total replay. She must have tripped over the path edge or something, and in an almost slow motion fashion she was heading down the bank; it seemed slow enough that I could have leapt forward and caught her. But I didn't. I was so blind with rage still that I couldn't process what was happening, couldn't make out what she yelled back. It wasn't 'till she was gone, over the edge, that I made my way down the bank. I'm pleased to say that I did run, and I did hope that she would be hanging on. But I'm sure you've guessed that she was gone. The most vivid image I have of that day is her body, almost naked, crashed onto the rocks, limbs at angles they shouldn't be at. I couldn't even see her head, there were just fragments of red here and there, scattered across the rocks. Her body heaved up and down; it looked like she was breathing, but it was just the movement of the waves."

Cpt Finn broke out into a reserved sobbing, he could not fully restrain the emotion any longer, but by no means did he unleash his full sorrow. He slumped forward and held his head in his grubby, uninjured hand. The hairs on the back of his paw were darkened by grime and had caught small fragments of debris which stood up like dandelions in a thick meadow; the mass of black stood out with great contrast against the pale skin beneath, glistening with stale sweat. A distended blue vein shone through the matting, like a bird's eye view of a river through a thick forest canopy.

Myers remained still, not knowing what else to do. Feeling somewhat awkward and out of place, he held his breaths occasionally, trying to keep quiet and draw as little attention to himself as possible, hoping he might just be able to become camouflaged from sight and sink into the shadows. With an obvious lump in his throat, Cpt Finn spoke once again, his head still dropped in his hand.

"I never forgave her. I never said I was sorry" his sentences were becoming broken "I never... never got to say goodbye. I enlisted in the army on the declaration of war, with full intention of going to the front line. I rose up because it was apparent I was *brave*" there was a sardonic quality to his words "turns out there's a thin line between bravery and suicidal tendencies. I lost count of how many times I've hoped that a bullet would come sailing through my skull. I can't do it to myself. But if I die in the field, then I can go and be with them..." He trailed off towards the end, his monologue becoming more pensive and personal.

"Then there was you, my boy" Cpt Finn finally turned to face Myers, who suddenly had a look of trepidation upon his face, fearing what was to be said or done. "I saw something in you, and you inspired me." Myers gave a slight smirk, although inside he was beaming.

"You've done me proud, my boy" the grin was withdrawn from Myers' face as his eyes darted to the swollen hand of the captain, "I can only hope I've been a help to you, as you have me"

There was a moment of silence before Cpt Finn finished.

"When I dragged you to the floor, it was only because I was fearful; didn't want you being popped off" the characteristic tone of Cpt Finn had returned; he delivered the words, said through his gravely yet comforting voice, with an air of light-heartedness and jovial feel, so as to try and lift the dark mood that was killing any colour or brightness in the room.

Myers was overjoyed with the acceptance from his father figure, and found his hearing muffled and eye sight blurred, along with a reserved childish grin across his immature face. He gave a slight flinch, then wiped his face with the back of his hand.

Cpt Finn let out a barking howl that echoed off the concrete pillars of the room. Myers shook himself to find that the captain had been shot through the foot. A second bullet had thrown up debris like an erupting geyser, which followed a lethargic choreography to settle on the surface film of the spreading crimson pool. Myers leapt to his feet and dragged the captain over to where he had been sitting, where the positioning of pillars and the glassless window frames was such so as to block line of sight with the tower block completely, where they were both fairly sure the shooter was. A second shot was fired, which this time Myers was alert enough to take note of. The bullet hit the floor, chipping up a fragment of grey concrete, partly shrouding the surrounding floor with dust; the event, seemingly in slow motion, took place momentarily before the pop of the shot was heard, ricocheting between the standing buildings dotted around the square. Cpt Finn gave short, sharp grunts through teeth gritted hard to the point of fracture, with his eyes screwed up as tight as they could be. Myers was in a state of panic and breathed heavy and fast, his head bobbing this way and that in confusion and worry. His eyes stood out, wide open, like golf balls stuck to the front of his cold, sweating face. There was a trail of blood across the floor, resembling a patchy brush stroke on a blank canvas. Myers was still immobile, looking helpless with his mouth open at Cpt Finn.

"I'll draw his..." Cpt Finn started, before having to convulse slightly, then recomposing himself "...draw his fire. You look, then shoot" he had to give crude instructions to conserve breath and be able to iterate his thoughts between moments of crippling agony. The information was lacking in detail and left Myers having to think for an extra moment to understand how to go about tackling the threat.

"I can't shoot straight..." again a convulsion from the captain, trying to absorb the throbbing pain emanating from his left foot "the flash will give his position..." he broke off and did not continue. The captain had screwed up his face, exaggerating the creases already present.

With tight lips Myers nodded, showing his understanding of what Cpt Finn had meant, and he squinted his eyes just slightly, feeling it radiated an air of control and composure, not that Cpt Finn was paying attention to what Myers was trying to show.

"Wait!" Cpt Finn snapped out of his trance-like state with a start "load my rifle!... just in case" Myers immediately heeded the instructions and raced to ready the Lee Enfield, drawing a bullet into the breach; he was awestruck at the silky, lubricated action of the slide, having never felt a mechanism so crisp before or heard such a sweet sound of two metal pieces gliding over one another, separated by a minute film of lubricating liquid which sounded like melted chocolate being folded over with a wooden spoon; he almost had a lust to perform the action again.

"Now boy, c'mon! Hand it here!" Cpt Finn had a single arm outstretched, reaching for *his* rifle.

Myers thrust the rifle into Cpt Finn's arm, almost regretfully letting go of it. A brief word from the captain and Myers ran towards the stairs in the far corner of the room, not bothering to keep low, so that he could run faster in an attempt to avoid an enemy bullet. A shot was fired, ricocheting behind Myers' heel and puffing up a gritty cloud, and almost too quickly a second shot hit the floor just ahead of Myers.

The stair case would break line of sight with the enemy sniper, and allow Myers to make his way to cover on the floor below and watch out for the enemy as Cpt Finn drew their fire. He raced down the stairs, light footed, skidded and turned about at the bottom and scanned the room for cover. The floor was laid out differently to above, having more diving walls, although still remaining fairly open and barren from any furnishings or colour. Myers quickly crept up behind one of the perimeter walls; he was adjacent to a window opening, free from any glass; not far beyond stood the tower block. He squatted with his back to the wall and checked his rifle was ready to go, the mechanicals feeling rusty and neglected after experiencing Cpt Finn's perfectly tuned tool. With the Lee Enfield clasped in his moist right hand, he fumbled to retrieve from his pack a small rectangular mirror on a thin telescopic arm, faintly pitted. Extending each of the three sections, which gave a soft grinding, he held up the mirror to look back over his head at the building in question. Holding it up to the corner of the window opening, he spied on the tower, although without the magnification of a scope, he couldn't check individual windows for the presence of the enemy; he would have to wait for a shot, acting like a signal flare against the light-sapping tower, which, even in the brightening sun, stood just as ominously dull as ever.

The thunderous crack of a shot resounded, and Myers recoiled into himself. A second shot followed.

TEN

For weeks he had sat up in the building, vigilant like a sailor atop the ship's mast. There was only reason to look out in the one direction; to the rear was Berlin, and there was no point watching over what was already taken care of. No, he was to look out away from Berlin, spy any enemy activity, and act. Using his large lensed binoculars, he would scan the horizon. He would survey the more immediate area, the derelict and rubble strewn streets, simply with his crisp eyesight, keen as the eagle of the German empire.

His Walther Gewehr 43 sniper rifle was never far from hand should something be spied. On a weekly basis he would disassemble the rifle and painstakingly clean and lubricate the mechanism with an oily yet somehow grit free rag, before methodically rebuilding the rifle and testing the mechanism for its satisfying mechanical clunks. He felt like a watch maker, building precision pieces of engineering and finding satisfaction from the 'ticks' and 'tocks' his work inevitably produced.

In weeks and months gone by, he had removed silhouettes from the horizon like a master artist removing blots from his canvas. He took sadistic pleasure in glaring down the scope into the face of his prey, but his targets were often at too great a distance to able to distinguish facial features. They were rarely too far away for the copper glazed bullets though. On many occasions he had fired a shot into the middle of a group of enemy soldiers, dropping one man who would fall on his knees into muddy ground before slowly toppling forward to bury his face in the earth. The remnants of the group always scattered in random directions, frantically trying to find cover. The self-loading action of the rifle allowed him to continue to fire without hesitation; ten shots as quickly as he could pull the smooth blade of the trigger. The quickness of the incoming metal slugs always instilled that bit more fear into his prey. One or two of the targets might not be fully hidden, gifting him a free shot. If he was fortunate, a soldier may even exhibit their head as they try and seek out the enemy shooter. A single bullet would rock back the head violently and produce a trail of red mist on its exit before the sound of the shot even reached the falling body.

He had earned quite the reputation, both among peers and enemy alike, and he loved both the praise and fear associated with his name. The thought brought a wry smirk to his aging face, creased heavily and ingrained with grime. His blonde hair had thinned much over the years and his body had faded from the formerly healthy plump figure. But his blue eyes were as sharp as the long knife he had secured in a leather sheath at his belt.

***

He was taking a break from the laborious scanning of the area, which was acceptable to do for about an hour; no one could cover the distance that his field of vision granted before he resumed his surveying. But an outburst nearby in the enemy's tongue forced his eyes open. He scrambled from his laid back position against a pillar; a soiled seat cushion had been offering luxurious comfort in the lonely building. Clutching his rifle, he made his way to a section of wall between two windows. He lent with his right shoulder against the masonry, the afternoon sun sitting just right in the sky to leave the area where he stood in shadow. It sounded like it was from the square. *But how has anyone slipped by?* He irately thought to himself.

He scanned the area frantically, trying to force his uncharacteristic self-annoyance out of his mind. He knew what he had heard, and he wouldn't cease his observation until he had found the source. Absolute patience was one of the many traits that made him a formidable sniper. He took a step back into the deeper shadow of the room and planted his unpolished boots in a steady stance, ready to endure the wait while he searched.

It wasn't long. He heard a dull thud and was able to narrow his search to the building ahead and to the left, one of the buildings along the edge of the square opposite. He supposed the uninvited company was here specifically for *him*, not that it bothered him; it added to the excitement, if anything. He knew which building would offer the best shooting vantage against his tower block; he had made a half attempt at sealing the building to prevent such, but like the lacklustre sheen of his boots and the scattered mess that was his living quarters, he had made little commitment to the task. One the few things he did fully commit to, however, was rifle maintenance and use thereof.

He scanned the suspected building, first with his naked eye, second with the magnification of the rifle scope, his left eye tightly shutting out the light while his right was locked open, unblinking, staring down the crisp scope lenses, free from any grime. The magnification was too high, being set for long distance shooting, making the task less efficient. The scope was perfectly set at its high magnification, so he refrained from adjusting the settings for fear of not having sufficient time to reset the scope.

He persevered. Eventually, he lowered the barrel, the butt still pressed hard into his shoulder, and once again eyed the building. A figure darted across his vision. Like a shot, the barrel was raised and he looked fiercely down the scope. The first thing he saw was a pair of black boots, muddied at the sole. He squeezed the trigger once. Twice. Two shots in rapid succession; no clunky reloads required after each ejection of a bullet. He watched with tunnel vision as the first bullet punched through the thick leather; the second bullet impacted the grey floor, kicking up dust that caught the yellow of the sun's rays. He was dissatisfied though; the scope was at too high a magnification. He couldn't aim effectively.

Time elapsed, yet he stood patient. Eventually a figure ran from right to left pf his vision. Again, he teased the trigger, once, twice. Both misses.

He quietly cursed and lowered the rifle as the figure disappeared from his scoped vision. He slid behind the cover of the wall and quickly made to adjust his sights. He twisted the barrel of the scope, shifting the positioning of the lenses to allow him to aim effectively at the required distances. To ensure a crisp calibration, he pivoted to a window directly to his left. Looking through his adjusted sights, he selected a dusty half-brick which lay against the background of the muted colours of a cobbled road. He positioned the crosshairs on the top left corner of the brick, and squeezed the trigger. The shot reverberated around the empty square and the echoes sounded a series of fainter cracks. The noise didn't matter; the enemy already knew he was here.

The recoil kicked back his shoulder slightly, but his gaze was held fast and he watched as the bullet kicked up a cloud of dust from where he *hadn't* aimed. Quickly, he lowered the rifle and removed the dull black dust caps that allowed him to adjust the crosshair positioning. He abruptly repeated his test shot, this time fracturing the brick and sending a spurt of rich, red fragments a short distance into the atmosphere.

He was ready to dispose of the vermin.

***

"Myers, can you hear me?" Cpt Finn said in a controlled bellow.

A short, panicked 'yelp' was the response.

"I'm going to make a diversion. Use your mirror to look for the shooter." Cpt Finn paused, catching his breath and closing his tired eyes. "You'll need to be fast to get a shot in yourself"

"Okay" was simply the response.

***

He glowered down the scope, absolutely clear but for stray foreign specs caught in the periphery of the lens. His breathing was heavy and rhythmic as he slowly swept the building, left to right, right to left.

Geduld, he iterated to himself, *patience.*

Then there it was; a clumsy section of tweed, spilling out from the back of a concrete pillar. There was no hesitation; the rifle already cocked and eager to fire, a smooth tug at the trigger and the copper coated lead slug was spat from the barrel ahead of a burst of fiery light and an ear splitting clap. He continued to stare down the length of the scope, with a greedy lust, desperate to see blood spill from flesh. But his gaze turned to confusion, as the tweed of the enemy did not bleed. Maybe he *had* been impatient. He leered once more, stealing a quick glance without the aid of the rifle scope as well, trying to be sure. He knew for certain his aim was true. The impact was clear; the ripples radiating across the fabric, particles being wheezed out from the dust trapped within the weave. There was no mistaking though; the object did not bleed.

***

The shot made Myers flinch.

Cpt Finn! His immediate startled thought ran to the injured captain. He knew better than to call out, so he strained to listen for anything suggesting life from above. But he could not hear anything, although not aided by the impairing throbbing heartbeat in his ears.

Worst of all, he hadn't even seen the muzzle flash in his mirror. Angry at himself, he whipped the mirror back and forth in a desperate manner, crudely inspecting windows, like ominous back alleys, disappearing into un-wandered depths of a crooked town. His chin was clenched hard to the point of hurting his teeth and he desperately willed the lump in his throat to fade away. There was determination in his heart but no focus in his eyes as he scanned and searched, panicked.

***

Cpt Finn had edged his rucksack across the coarse, leaden floor, which clawed at the fabric to leave fine tendrils in the wake of the sack. He made every effort to give purposeful carelessness to the action, so as to any onlookers it appeared someone had unintentionally revealed a small portion of themselves to be taken advantage of.

Almost as the finest sliver of the canvas had peered round the pillar, the rucksack jolted back as the bullet struck with a thud, scattering particles like confetti into the local atmosphere. The sharp crack from the rifle echoed round the room as though trapped.

The decoy worked, he thought. Except only a solitary crack had whistled through the air. Myers had missed his opportunity.

Cpt Finn's eyelids sagged as he released a heavy sigh. He felt cold and weary in the stark space and longed to feel warmth swell over him.

They remained pinned down. Cpt Finn exhaustively ran through scenario after scenario, and kept finding himself back at needing to draw more fire from the enemy. The added issue which presented itself in his calculations was that a simple lifeless decoy wouldn't work anymore; the sniper would most certainly wait until he knew what he was loosing off bullets towards.

"Myers!" he mustered the energy to bark, "I'm going to have to draw fire again. Same plan. Spot the muzzle flash, and shoot!" there was an intimation of reserved frustration underpinning his words.

A muffled response from Cpl Myers cantered through the dense air to reach Cpt Finn as he worked to stand, leaning his back hard into the pillar as he ascended to his feet. He felt his tendons strain as he heaved the rifle to cradle it between his hands, only it slipped straight through his injured palm, the wound having become agonisingly tender. Involuntarily, he took a sharp inhale through gritted teeth and temporarily shut out the muted light of the room with eyelids screwed so tightly shut not even a single tear could leak past.

He stood straight and recomposed himself. He outstretched the forearm of his injured hand, providing a platform on which he could rest the rifle. It wasn't ideal, he thought to himself, but he didn't need precision aiming.

He slowed his breathing, and a concentration washed over his grime ridden features to the point he looked emotionless.

He stepped out from the behind the pillar, gun raised and aimed in the general direction of the tower block, and yanked the trigger. A bullet was spat, twisting in a fiery blaze, from the end of the barrel. The recoil hit Cpt Finn like a horse had bucked him in the shoulder and he was forced to take a step back and balance himself before he retreated to the safety of the pillar.

No returning shot

He needed to reload and repeat. Quickly, he lowered the end of the barrel to the floor and gripped it between his feet, allowing him to action the slide with his trigger hand. A clunk and a click, and he was ready once more.

***

With a mixture of desperation and determination on his face, Myers glared at the reflection of the tower block, angled the mirror this way and that in an attempt to scan every window.

Cpt Finn made his shot. But no flares of light from returning fire.

Obediently he remained vigilant. He knew Cpt Finn wasn't finished yet.

***

Cpt Finn took a lungful of the gritty air before stepping out to the opposite side of the pillar and once more let loose a bullet to sail unguided towards the leaden mass of the tower.

He swung back behind the pillar and reloaded again, all the while listening between the tinny echoes for the emergence of an out of place crack. But nothing came. The plan wasn't working, a different attack was required.

Cpt Finn gently closed his eyes and breathed deeply and rhythmically with the rifle still pointing to the earth between his cold feet. The faintest hint of a smile radiated on his face, the moist corners of his mouth becoming subtlety upturned and the diverging creases from his eyes distorting and creating marginally deeper ridges.

Reluctantly, he opened his eyes and stepped out from behind the pillar. Purposefully, he tried to take aim, clumsily peering down the scope of the rifle at the higher windows of the tower; it was the most likely area the sniper was going to be.

Then he saw it.

The flash of light.

And felt it.

The warmth in his chest.

He stumbled back and fell to the concrete floor, keeping his rifle cradled on top of him so as to protect it. He hit the cold ground and let out a sigh. He simply lay there with his eyes open to the changing light of the room. An effulgent yellow emanated from the stairwell at the corner of the room and seemed to highlight the softest azure imprisoned within the stone of the walls. Crystal flecks in the floor were slowly covered by an amorphous maroon pool stretching out from the captain. The ruby on his cheeks seemed to diminish with the increasing saturation on the ground around him. His eyelids drew to a close and the slightest smile formed across his face; from the moist corners of his eyes, more than simply a single tear coursed down the valley-like creases in his face, making their way to the red sea on which he floated away.

***

There it is! Myers caught the flash. He discarded the mirror and reverted to his rifle scope. He peered down the lens, ignoring the detritus collected at the periphery of the image. He had the window the flash came from in view, but no sight of a sniper. He was still stood back and to the side of the window obscuring any direct view for Myers.

This presented a difficult situation for Myers, as he could not move to gain a better view for risk of being seen, but sitting there waiting for the enemy to possibly come into view seemed an equally flawed option.

He remained still for a short while, not sure on the best approach, before another flash illumined the deep set window frame, the white hot colour brilliantly reflecting off the grey structure.

ELEVEN

A shot was fired.

He did not feel the warm metal though. Or hear the icy crack of a ricochet. The screaming lonely silence was broken, and with it came on a spell of self-preserving agoraphobia; desperate for sanctuary, he scrambled into the tower through a roughly barricaded entrance.

The space was starved of natural light, with small windows and numerous dividing walls. Long veneered desks were strewn about like pinecones on a concrete forest floor, and phones, papers and desk lamps littered the ground like leaf fall. There was an obvious disturbance to the chaotic debris which stood out of place like polished shoes in a quarry; a trail of disturbed brick dust and kicked-aside objects highlighted a route up the stairs, straight ahead of where he stood. With no better plan, Westfield followed the trail, slowly, up the stairs. He removed the revolver from the rucksack and rotated the cylinder, which gave soft clicks as the lone piece of metal was sent on a cyclic journey; one bullet was better than none.

He was thankful of the use of concrete for the construction of the stairs. *No creaks to give away position,* he thought. If there was one thing he absolutely needed in his arsenal, it was the element of surprise. A single bullet wasn't much good in an all guns blazing firefight.

Each floor he came to was mostly open plan, allowing him to make quick surveys and assess if all was clear.

Another shot. The noise flew around the cavernous space like a swarm of angered wasps. The shots were actually welcome news for Westfield; it meant the foe was pre-occupied, hopefully to the point where an approaching predator would not be sensed.

A third shot. Something was definitely going on out there. A sudden weight of concern bore down on his shoulders as he came to the realisation that his own countrymen could well be on the receiving end of this fire.

He quickened his pace and ascended two stairs at a time, although trod delicately to limit noise from crushing or skidding debris underfoot. Another shot sounded and was only a few more floors up, if that. He wound back his carefully hasty approach and continued towards the danger with a hunched stance, subconsciously feeling doing so reduced his emanation of noise.

With his ascension to each new unexplored floor he scanned the space cautiously from the stairwell, squinting to the far reaches of the room holding his breath whilst desperately listening for movement. Nothing. He continued to the next floor.

He reached the top of the flight of stairs as another shot resounded around the walls and pillars, like thick plate glass being attacked with hammers and axes. He was taken aback by the sheer volume in the baron area and felt dazed, just about managing to stand but unable to focus his gaze, his surroundings shimmering like a clashed cymbal. He blinked sporadically and raised a dry and worn hand to steady his head. His grip on the revolver, intertwined with his other hand, firmed slightly as from the depths of his blurred vision emerged a silhouetted frame.

***

The emerging image before Westfield sent an injection of adrenaline through his veins, sharpening his eyesight and tuning his ears. He raised the gun to chest height, held in both hands, and began edging forward, delicately. The silhouetted figure was still preoccupied with whatever was going on outside, conveniently distracted.

He crept gingerly towards the foe, inspecting where his next footfall was to go, picking his way through the gritty landscape. *Silence*. He had to remain silent.

He was just a few steps behind the enemy sniper. He took a final breath, so slowly that he needed to exhale again before his lungs had even been brimmed with the stale air. Fighting all reflexes to breathe, he steadied his aim at the back if the head of his prey and teased the trigger.

With conflagrant lungs he pulled the trigger to release a slug of burning lead through the acrid atmosphere.

There was a metallic click, but no explosive crack. No bullet fired. No man fell.

In a bemused panic, Westfield yanked at the trigger again. Once more there was only the ricocheting sound of the firing hammer coming to its sharp rest.

The German sniper had begun a pirouette on his tired heels, the cumbersome rifle clutched in his arms slowing his movements.

Westfield's eyelids seemed to recede entirely into his head and his pupils dilated as fear coursed through his system. Once more he pulled the trigger. Once more, nothing.

In desperation, the sniper pulled the trigger of his own weapon whilst he was mid-turn, trying to startle his foe and buy himself precious time. The noise was immense, leaving Westfield with high pitched alarm bells ringing in his ears, and the incandescence of the muzzle flash burnt an abstract image onto his vision.

Westfield yanked at the trigger again, imploring the revolver to spit its payload. He could not hear the clap of a shot for his tinnitus, but the lack of feedback into his hand told him no bullet had fired.

The sniper had advanced towards Westfield, rifle secured into his shoulder. The reverberation of a shot penetrated the muted hearing of Westfield, telling him he'd finally let loose his lone lump of lead. The sniper took a stumble backwards and fired a round as he involuntarily grasped at the trigger of the rifle. He clamped his other hand to the wound on his neck, which in seconds was stained profusely with blood.

The sniper started towards Westfield, dragging the barrel of his rifle along the pitted floor as though he was physically incapable of releasing it from his grip; an unnatural and eerie gargling noise emanated from the stricken soldier. In a panic, Westfield hurled the spent revolver at the approaching foe, which glanced off the snipers jaw, kicking his head to the side and forcing a grunt, but not ceasing his advancement.

Westfield stole a glance just over the shoulder of the sniper at the aurora-like glow emanating from the aperture in the wall to outside. His focus shot back to the sniper and his eyes and chin tightened. He thrust himself forward, automatically roaring as he connected his shoulder with the sniper's chest. He used his momentum to power the sniper backwards, who stumbled and spat bubbles of deep red blood which burst at the top of Westfield's spine to create a faint latticework which spread down his back. He pushed and yelled, his feet skidding occasionally on the loose floor scattering. The sniper finally released his grip on the rifle and hammered on the back of the Westfield's head.

Blocking all pain in his head and his hand, he gave a final shove, sending the sniper tripping backwards over the window ledge.

***

Myers remained locked on his scoped view of the window, confused by what was happening. He called out to Cpt Finn for any information, but he mustn't have heard as he did not receive a response.

Then a figure appeared at the window. *The sniper!* He began squeezing the trigger, but was stopped by his curiosity at letting the events before him unfold.

The sniper had fallen, or been pushed, from one of the windows. Except, he hadn't continued to fall; he had a grip on another man, who was evidently an allied soldier from his uniform and general appearance.

The allied soldier howled and grimaced as the enemy sniper clutched onto what appeared to be an injured hand. The sniper did not hold on with both hands though, his remaining hand being clamped to his throat.

The screams loudened as the allied soldier beat on the arm of the sniper, catching his barely congealed wound occasionally in his frenzy to be rid of the parasitic creature clinging onto life.

Myers moved his crosshairs delicately into position and forced all background colours and textures to sink away, focussing on his target, highlighted against the amorphous surroundings. He took a short breath and slowly squeezed the trigger.

The shimmering bullet grazed the forearm of the sniper and impacted the tower block, sending an explosion of fine dust into the face of the sniper which adhered to the blood smeared on his hand and neck like ash settling onto molten lava. The sniper roared and writhed involuntarily, but remained clung to the allied soldier like a fish caught on the end of a line. His hand which had been fastened to his neck wound slipped in the motions and rich strawberry coloured fluid percolated through his slightly parted fingers.

Still staring down the scope, Myers brought another bullet into the breach of the rifle. Again, he made a small inhalation, held his breath to reduce the sway of his crosshairs and pulled the trigger once more. The action was becoming much more second nature.

The copper glazed projectile was forced down the barrel of the rifle by the blistering expansion of unstable gunpowder. Twisting gently, it exited the darkness of the barrel into the blinding light of the day, breaking away from the caressing grasp of the intense fingers of flame. Effortlessly, it punched through the atmosphere, seemingly halting the passage of time: the supple beating of insect wings became stiff and lethargic; falling dust from a window ledge floated mid-air, caught by invisible netting; the trickle of coagulating blood on a hand was momentarily frozen, left to bake under the sun.

The flow of time reset as the bullet ripped clean through the forearm of the sniper, before being lost in the endless concrete of the tower block. Teardrops of saliva were shot from the sniper's mouth unwittingly as he gave an unearthly guttural scream. The residual flesh of his forearm began to rip, like the threads of a torn canvas sack finally unravelling, forming lengthening tendrils futilely bridging the expanding gap. In a desperate moment of paradoxical self-preservation he released the life sustaining grip on his neck wound and reached upwards for anything to preclude a fall to the barren streets below.

The sniper grabbed his own severed arm, still holding the allied soldier. Myers continued to watch the events unfold as the sniper's grip failed him, his bloodied hand skidding down the lifeless structure, brushing the newly frayed end of his forearm before he began his acceleration toward the strewn stone and concrete lying at the base of the tower, warmed by the scattered sunlight.

Myers retracted from the scope of the rifle, a slight look of bewilderment upon his aged face, and quickly looked out through a window to the streets below. A gentle waltz of dust took place over a localised space, almost obscuring the shifting shades of the arid ground below.

Myers raised his gaze to find the allied soldier in a daze, the severed limb still clamped onto him; the soldier returned from his trance and flicked the arm away in an erratic spasm of his hand, as though it were a phobia inducing item he wanted rid of.

"Hello!!" called Myers across the choking air distancing the two buildings.

The allied soldier looked with bewilderment over towards Myers, who almost felt the rush from his weighted sigh of relief. Short hand gestures were excitedly exchanged between the two men as they arranged to convene in the derelict strewn square.

Myers backed away from the window and ensured he had everything. Cpt Finn suddenly came into his mind; he had been so focussed on the events unfolding his thoughts had not stretched to the Captain. He raced to the level where Cpt Finn was, but stopped abruptly at the top of the grey stairs.

He strained to swallow as his throat closed. He stepped slowly towards the captain lying on his back, his rifle across his blood soaked chest. Myers did not bother to feel for a pulse; the copious amounts of red liquid painted the conclusion clearly enough.

Myers' gaze moved from the closed eyes of the captain, to the infinitely deep red pocket in his chest, to the clean and well serviced rifle. He leered uncontrollably, with a hint of lust, at the rifle, held so loosely by the dead man at his feet. He reached out and touched the smooth, weathered stock, ran his fingers gently along the fingerprints of the wood grain.

He retrieved the slightly mottled dog tags from around Cpt Finn's neck and reached into the captain's rucksack and pulled from it a neatly folded blanket; he laid a comforting hand on the captain's shoulder before draping the bobbled fabric over the body and rifle.

With his jaw clamped shut to stem any quivering, he stood, saluted, and walked away from the captain.

TWELVE

Cpl Myers forced his way through a barricaded window of the building to meet Sgt. Westfield, who stood waiting in the dying late afternoon sun. A relieved smile swept over Westfield's face as he introduced himself. Myers returned the pleasantries, although his expression remained hard and featureless.

"We need to get out of here" Myers authoritatively stated, "I'll radio back home and get us an evac"

Westfield was a little taken aback at the cold, aggressive tone, but let it slide. As Myers retrieved the radio from his rucksack and proceeded to radio for help, Westfield turned around and started walking in a large circle, kicking yellow dust into the stale air and scattering small pebbles which danced to a random pattering. He half-listened to some sort of altercation, trying not to appear as though he was encroaching on the Corporals increasingly heated words.

"The target has been eliminated… I have lost my commanding officer… I have an injured ally with me…" Myers barraged the person on the receiving end of the radio with all the justification he could stir up in an attempt he could win a plane ticket home.

"We will be there! Over and out" Myers began to repack the radio in his sack as he gave Westfield the news, "We leave tonight"

He subsequently retrieved a map from a side pocket which had surprisingly crisp and white edges. Westfield hurried to Myers and remained silent as the corporal continued.

"Pickup coordinates are here" he stated, prodding the map with a dry and cracked finger. "It's not close. We need to move now"

Westfield grunted in agreement.

As a last task before leaving the area, Myers hurriedly made his way to the fallen German sniper and snatched the dog tags from around his neck. The corners of his mouth curled towards the ground as he looked down at the crumpled form with disdain. He fought back the urge to deposit a glob of saliva on the corpse, instead settling for a restrained kicking of the ground, sending a soft shower of grit to precipitate on the body.

Myers turned and stormed away, clutching the straps of his rucksack in a defensive hunch. He neither uttered a word nor cast his thunderous face upon Westfield as he marched on past and up towards the rubble strewn streets he had walked not long before, a much more innocent boy.

Westfield started after the Corporal, quickly making up the lost ground to march by his side. He struggled for a few streets to make broken, one-sided conversation, before giving up entirely, forced to endure the tinnitus inducing incessant echoing of their boots pattering the cobbled ground.

***

They walked on an on. Hour after hour. But both men were thankful for the boredom, though. The last thing they wanted now was anything *eventful*.

They had left the bustle of the town for more rural land. The occasional house blotted the landscape canvas, woven with pastel fields and winding roads.

The quick march remained uneventful, and somewhat silent; forced exchanges of conversation had taken place like fits of oppressive gunfire, but these soon fizzled out to leave only the unsynchronised tick-tock of heavy footfall as time relentlessly continued at a seemingly slowing pace.

Myers powered ahead, being the only carrier of a weapon, very occasionally glancing back at his wounded ally, turning his whole body sideways as he did so due to the restriction of his rucksack.

The only time they stopped was to re-consult the map or when potential threats were spotted, the latter acting to hinder their progress further. The sun continued its smooth transit across the altocumulus strewn sky, the light gradually brightening and dimming behind the pocked mask of clouds. Ever reddening shadows were cast across the undulating ground as the dying light desperately writhed its way over opaque masses.

An epoch seemed to drift by. With blistered feet and little energy, still they marched.

They arrived at the specified coordinates; an expanse of flat, open ground, good enough to act as a temporary runway. Under the protective speckled blanket of the night sky, they stayed low to the fast-cooling earth and waited for the burble of propeller blades slicing through the atmosphere.

***

"Hear that!?" Westfield barely broke the eternal silence with his hushed, hurried question. He glanced at Myers, then stood to search the sky.

Myers slowly rose to his feet, not wanting to make any noise. He turned his head in a strained effort to listen for salvation. And there is was. Subtly cutting through the rustling night time foliage and whispers of insects.

"Keep an eye out. We're going to have to run. They're not waiting for us" Myers stated in a hushed voice.

Westfield made no attempt to reply. He continued to scan the sky, eyes squinted in a hope it'd allow him to see further. The bumble got louder, but still neither man could see the source of the noise. The engine surged occasionally as the aircraft was buffeted by cross winds, forcing the pilot to demand more power and keep the craft on a true course.

"There!" Westfield bellowed, unable to contain his euphoria.

The plane was mere metres off the ground, flown in with no landing lights to reduce the risk of being spotted. Immediately Westfield and Myers began their charge, tearing across the stretch of open fields ahead of them in an attempt to intercept the trajectory of the aircraft.

The plane hit the ground, hard, the spring of the undercarriage resisting the impact and acting to force the craft momentarily back into the air; like a stone skimming the surface of a rippled pond, the plane hopped across in front of Westfield and Myers before slowing to the pace of a brisk walk, the tailfin nodding as the aberrations in the makeshift runway were traversed.

A soft shaft of crimson light appeared on the ground; the opened door in the side of the fuselage invited the two soldiers on board. Westfield and Myers pounded the ground, chasing after the blood red aperture.

Westfield reached the plane first, aided by not being weighed down by any equipment. He ran alongside the craft, reached in through the door to grasp a handle and hauled himself in. He turned and crouched in the doorway, one hand fastened to a grab rail, his injured hand stretched out the door.

"Take my arm!" Westfield yelled over the engine drone, so much louder once inside the tinny innards of the place.

"Lose the equipment! Just grab my arm!"

Myers was past the rear of the aircraft, but making slow progress to the door. His breathing was as heavy as his footfalls, his arms pumped the turbulent air while his rucksack, with rifle jutting out the top, danced erratically on his back.

"We're running out of time here. He needs to be on board now" the order was barked from the front of the plane, "We can't afford to stop"

Westfield swung himself out the plane as much as possible to extend his reach. His knuckles quickly transitioned to an alabaster hue as he was forced to tighten his grip on the rail with the undulations of the plane.

"Myers, lose the stuff. Now!"

Myers continued to run, repositioning his rucksack in awkward, stuttered movements. He clutched the rifle and let the rucksack drop to the ground, almost tripping over it as the weighty canvas fell to the spongy ground. His pace quickened and he approached the outstretched arm of Westfield.

"That's it. We're out of runway. I'm taking her up!" the co-pilot bellowed.

The burble of the engines became a roar. Westfield strained to reach further towards the back of the plane, his grip on the handle being reduced to only his fingertips. In the momentary delay between the engines sucking in more air and the propellers cutting the atmosphere into thinner slices, Myers lunged forward, grasping the wounded hand of Westfield, a thin crust of coagulated blood being broken to reveal the sticky sublayer.

Westfield winced and screamed and shuddered, but did not retract his arm from the source of the pain. He tried to tighten his grip on the hand of Myers, but could not will his injured hand to muster any usable strength. He slowly retracted his arm towards the opening of the plane, bringing Myers with it.

The plane had begun to gather speed, Myers' feet now dancing across the makeshift runway in random skips, no longer able to keep pace with the groundspeed of the aircraft, his legs flailing like a ragdoll. With regret, Myers threw his rifle through the plane door, which clattered across the steel clad flooring, scuffing the lacquered woodwork of the weapon. With his newly freed hand, he grasped the upper arm of Westfield and managed to hoist himself up from the ground. He placed a battered foot on the fuselage of the plane and pushed, levering himself round and almost through the plane door. With a final agonising haul, Westfield brought Myers crashing through the aperture to land in a heap in the middle of the plane. Westfield fell to the floor, his hand still unconsciously gripping the handrail, the wrinkled skin of his hands pulled taught over his knuckles, bereft of any colour. Beads of sweat glinted in the soft red light.

Myers got to his feet in laboured movements, not aided by the jostling of the plane as it left the spongy ground and climbed steeply to reach its cruising altitude. He retrieved his rifle, which had been flitting around the cabin space, before sitting on the floor at the side of the plane. He made a short glance at Westfield and offered a sharp nod, then turned his cold expression towards the mixture of metal and wood cradled in his arms.

After a few minutes the plane levelled off. The wind rushed past the still open door, whistling a non-melodic tune, unappreciated by the tired audience. A figure emerged from the cockpit, presumably the co-pilot, thought Myers. He walked to the turbulent aperture and slid the door shut, ceasing the relentless buffeting assault on the ears.

"I am Major Hatton" the figure stated plainly.

He moved his hairless head, concealed by a beret, from one side of the plane to the other, assessing his newly boarded cargo. He stood with his legs apart and hands locked behind his back, his frame rigid and unwavering against the shudders of the aircraft.

Both Myers and Westfield queried to themselves the reason for a senior officer to be present on this collection mission. A cold chill spread through their guts.

"We have been sent to collect you following your mission success" Mjr Hatton began, a sense of impending bad news in his tone.

"I'm afraid you're skills, both of you", once again, his deep set eyes scanned across the plane, "are still required. You're not off home just yet"

Myers and Westfield had been bracing for some ill-wanted information, although it was still a blow to actually hear the words. Neither man said anything; they sat in silence and continued to listen, not that they had a choice.

"Very recently we received intelligence giving almost certainty to Hitler's location. He has a retreat situated in the Alps; Berghof" Hatton paused and glanced round his audience, expecting a more lively reaction than he received.

"We shall need to embellish the plan" he continued in a stiff monotone drone that occasionally was lost behind the omnipresent reverberations of the aircraft, "although the basis is to enter the building under disguise of a German officer and eliminate Adolf Hitler. We understand there is a large gathering of high ranking officials taking place, providing enough bodies to be able to blend in and be forgotten about, to hide in plain sight".

Both Myers and Westfield were aghast. Both sat on the hellish cold steel floor under the searing burning red of the tungsten bulbs above them.

"Sergeant Westfield?" Hatton looked in turn at each of the faces sat before him. Westfield gave a slight nod as Hatton's searchlight gaze fell upon him.

"I'm informed your German is very good. Is my information correct?"

"It is sir. I used to teach languages and was initially drafted as a translator" Westfield replied, his voice an addled mix of enthusiasm at his previously overlooked skill, and concern as to the path he was being dragged down.

"Excellent. It'll need to be good. You'll be passing yourself off an a Nazi officer" Hatton delivered the words so mundanely it was almost easy for Westfield to loose grip on the gravity of situation coming into focus before him; if he slipped up, he died.

"Intelligence has presented us with an almost unique opportunity which must be capitalised on, albeit at the expense of preparation" Hatton stonily enunciated the rehearsed line. It was unequivocal that a significant degree of improvisation and subterfuge would be required.

The operation was discussed at length as the plane burbled into the night. Alterations and concerns were volleyed back and forth between the three men. Their positions changed from sitting to standing to leaning, more and more often as they all became increasingly restless, the dance of moves seemingly being passed from man to man in a choreographed arrangement.

From the rear of the plane, equipment and supplies could be heard jangling and rustling as the plane jostled through turbulent pockets of the atmosphere. Amongst the equipment were two parachutes.

THIRTEEN

The chilled air whipped past Westfield's ears, sounding like a roaring waterfall as it hammers away at solid rock; the noise was relentless, almost enough to induce hysteria. The canvas sack containing his equipment was strapped to his front, the fabric rippling so quickly it looked alive. Through the gloom below him he could just make out Myers, falling to Earth with arms and legs outstretched in a star shape. There was nothing else to be seen, the landscape having the concealing cloak of nightfall draped over it.

As they continued to fall and the ground drew increasingly near, subtle shapes became discernible, emerging as slightly different shades of black silhouetted against the infinite backdrop.

Trees. Lots of trees.

Westfield blinked, and on reopening of his eyes found Myers had deployed his parachute and seemingly come to a halt as Westfield fell past. He didn't bother consulting the altitude meter on his wrist for fear of lack of time. His arms felt as though they were slicing through treacle as he reached for his ripcord, all the while the air becoming less icy as the ground grew larger with each sporadic glimpse.

He clenched his fingers so tightly around the fluttering handle of the ripcord that the weave of his gloves began to part across his tense knuckles. Desperately, he yanked and his parachute deployed, the arresting motion like a hammer blow to his body, throwing him into an upright position. With a quiet sigh of relief he began scouring the landscape, searching for a black hole in the darkness, a clearly in the tree canopy to touch down.

As the tree tops crept closer and closer, finally a clearing revealed itself from the murky mask, almost as a single candle illumining the exit from a cell bereft of any other light.

Wait, thought Westfield, *that clearing* is *lit! That's the access road!*

The trajectory of Westfield and Myers jump was intended to bring them close to Berghof, Hitler's alpine retreat; it wasn't supposed to put them *on* the road to their destination. The blackout headlights of the polished Daimler cast just enough light for the driver to see the road immediately ahead of him; if Westfield and Myers circled, slowing their descent, they could avoid being seen.

The two men delayed as much as possible, but ultimately they had to reconnect with the ground. The lack of light made landing for both men hard, each rolling across the dusty track on impact.

The hollow pops of an engine became audible against the ambient rustling of trees. Westfield and Myers made a quick glance to one another before gathering their parachutes and scurrying to the sheltering tree line edging the driveway.

Without hesitation Myers reached into his pack and produced a pistol and silencer. As he hurriedly assembled the parts, he sensed Westfield's gaze upon him.

"Getting you a ticket through the front door" he softly said, his eye line not breaking from the direction of the approaching vehicle.

With no alternative, Westfield deferentially agreed. Myers just had time to remove his parachute harness before he stepped into the middle of the track, his black attire nondescript. He stood with a firm stance, pistol wielding hand tucked behind his back, his other raised in a 'stop' gesture.

The regular, oppressive rattle of the vehicle's engine drew nearer, and very soon the subtle leaden hues of the road burst to life against the colourless background as the car rounded the corner ahead of Myers. The car came to a slow halt, the brakes giving a slight squeal as the vehicle pitched forward on the soft suspension. Even the blackout headlights resulted in a significant glare in the contrasting night. Surface aberrations cast very long shadows which crept like eerie fingers clawing at the boots of Myers.

With both hands now behind his back, giving a comfortable looking posture whilst actually acting to conceal his weapon, he made his way deliberately to the driver side of the vehicle. Ensuring he wasn't too close, he stooped slightly to be able to see into the vehicle as the driver rolled down the window. Three occupants.

"Guten Abend" Myers said with a polite smile.

Without awaiting a response, he threw his pistol out in front of himself and twisted his body in one fluid motion. One soft pop. A slight pause. A second attenuated explosion. Both the driver and front passenger slumped forward, a single headshot to each. The windscreen was peppered with small liquid beads, which left striations as they slowly streaked downwards.

He just saw the rear passenger clawing their way out of the rear door, on the opposite side to Myers; he made a swift side step, then squeezed the trigger. The bullet cut a clean hole in the rear side window and kissed the edge of the Italian leather before embedding in the rear of the escaping German's thigh. Through the spider web cracks and the small cloud of stuffing suspended in the air, Myers saw the passenger fall out of the vehicle, as though pushed.

From the treeline, Westfield watched as Myers hastily walked round to the opposite side of the vehicle; the headlight glare meant he could only make out his outline. The muted muzzle flash instantaneously illuminated the expressionless face of Myers with pastel yellow hues, before it receded back into the concealing darkness.

FOURTEEN

After obtaining the identification from one of the deceased officers, Westfield and Myers dragged the three bodies into the woods. Westfield removed his parachute harness and jumpsuit to reveal a German officer's uniform, not quite pressed to precision, but passable. What he didn't have, though, were a pair of the black gloves all of the vehicle occupants had; he forced his wounded hand into the largest of the gloves available, screwing up his eyes and nearly biting off his tongue as he did, the pain being like red hot needles shooting under his fingernails and spreading like wildfire to leave his whole hand a throbbing balloon, inflated to the point of rupture.

The jacket from one of the fallen had been screwed up into a ball and was used to wipe the car of traces of slaughter. The gelatinous liquid smeared across the windscreen before finally being collected by the absorbent cotton fibres on multiple passes. The exterior of the car was given the same treatment, although the natural darkening of the coagulating blood meant it almost complimented the black paintwork.

The car was still running as Westfield went to climb inside. Foggy fumes were spluttered from the chrome exhaust, picked out by the diffused red glow of the tail lights. Myers walked around to the driver's window as he tossed the spent jacket into the woods.

"I'll get in position" his tired vocal chords crackled like a dying fire. He collected his pack and headed just into the trees before commencing a brisk walk, following the sweep of the access road.

Westfield slotted the automatic gearbox into drive and smoothly pulled away. He spent a considerable proportion of time inspecting the plush interior of the vehicle. The polished wood of the dashboard, with the grain highlighted so clearly it looked three dimensional. The stark aroma of leather filled the cabin space so overwhelmingly Westfield was forced to leave the driver window down, which he operated with a satisfying clack of a toggle switch.

The drive was surprisingly far, with little break in the trees until the final corner was rounded and the impressive structure of Berghof, Hitler's alpine retreat, was upon Westfield. He made sure the side of the car with the bullet shattered window was kept out of view of the guards swarming around the building, manoeuvring the vehicle this way and that in a seemingly amateurish dance as he parked amongst the collection of entirely black high-end German vehicles.

He exited the vehicle and straightened his attire. Checked for his newfound identity. His polished boots looked bedraggled and gnarled in contrast to the sea of highly maintained metalwork he was standing around.

Without waiting to be asked, he presented the ID to one of the guards at the front of the building and introduced himself as Fredrick Weber. There was no smile or pleasantries as the guard relieved Westfield of the document. He wrestled in his mind with the thought of trying to make idle small talk, trying to distract the guards from over-scrutinising the stolen document, held between the warmth of a gloved hand and the cold of an automatic sub-machine gun. He decided against the idea, and remained stood in as confident a stance as he could muster, feet shoulder width apart, arms tucked behind his back and chin held strong and high.

An unnerving timeframe seemed to stutter by, and Westfield's brow was just beginning to mist with fine beads of perspiration, when the guard granted him access to the building.

"Do you need assistance with collecting bags from your vehicle, Mr Weber?" questioned one of the guards, inquisitive glances up and down being made at the lack of overnight baggage.

"Oh. No. Thank you" replied Westfield in perfect German, despite a difficult to place accent, "I am travelling light. Thank you again though".

Not a flawless excuse, he critiqued himself. He didn't wait for anything to be mulled over and authoritatively made motions to enter Berghof.

Inside, there was another pair of guards, framed against the backdrop of light wood panelling, standing so rigid they almost blended in with the art works adorning the walls of the entrance hall. Westfield gave a curt nod as he passed, unsure exactly what the protocol should be. He made sure not to question a decision once his mind was made. *Confident actions*, he thought.

In his effort to maintain an authoritative demeanour, he found himself strutting the length of corridors, following the flattened weave of the slightly tired looking carpet, turning corners where he could the break line of sight with any onlookers. Fortunately for Westfield, a tall, thin framed man appeared in front of him, not dressed in officer or guard uniform.

"Good evening" the man began, "may I direct you to the sleeping quarters, sir?" he enquired.

"Please. I fear I am fatigued from my journey" Westfield replied, the German words effortlessly rolled off his tongue.

In silence, Westfield followed the angular man, whose shoulders cut into the thin shirt he wore. Through a warren of walkways, the member of staff ceased his brisk walk, forced himself to stand upright and turned to Westfield; he gestured toward a dark stained door with a brass handle polished to a mirror-finish. Westfield began to thank the man but was cut off.

"There are refreshments available in the dining hall, should that be your wish" a cryptic list of directions to the hall followed, which Westfield struggled to comprehend; his mind was beginning to wander as his swollen hand throbbed, entombed by the seemingly ever shrinking leather glove.

"May I have your bags collected?" the man asked in his dry voice, clearly just noticing Westfield's lack of baggage.

"Oh. No. That's fine. Thank you" Westfield replied, deliberately keeping his response brief to save tripping over his own lies with some sort of cover story. He closed the door of his own cell before any response could follow.

Lethargically, he walked on wavering legs to the small sink on the opposite wall. He desperately tried to wash away the tired emotions on his face; apathy was all he wanted to display. He drew a sharp breath through gritted teeth as his swollen hand ran over the contours of his face, the pressure on the raw, cerise flesh shooting pain up his arm and neck. After sitting heavily onto the bed, he concluded the opportunity to get some nourishment in him would be beneficial.

Following as best a grooming as he could manage, he went to the mess hall and picked at the offerings of cold meats and bread. He exchanged reserved pleasantries with the few others late-night fuelling, but made sure not to be drawn into full blown conversation. He was sat at one of the numerous long, dark wood tables, the deep grain very slightly sticky with the infiltration of contaminants over the years, despite the frequent cleaning it must have received, judging from the pristineness of the cold tiled floor and how almost offensively bright and harsh the steel serving platters were.

He rose from his chair, as nondescript as possible, and returned to the serving area, where the offerings had fallen through their optimum temperature window with no hope of altering their pre-written outcome. Westfield reached for a single slice of stale bread, brittle to the point it required delicate handling, crumbs being shed like snow from a shaken tree. He collected a sachet of butter and a fresh set of cutlery and returned to his table.

As he began to sit, swinging his arms behind him to reach for the chair, he slipped the roll of cutlery into his jacket pocket. Pulling up his chair, he proceeded to butter the bread he did not want with a knife left on the table previously. He had no particular plan with the newly acquired dull instruments; it was merely an opportunistic move, acquiring a reserve piece in his chess game.

Having force fed himself the arid provisions, he rose, the chair legs squawking with alarm against the stony floor. With the assumption the only next action was to wait for morning, he exited for the terrace to indicate, with a surreptitious glance, to Myers that there wouldn't be an opportunity today.

As he stepped through the front door to the terrace, like reaching the exit of a tunnel with a train bearing down behind, its horn blasts muffled by the pulsing blood through ears, a hand gripped Westfield's shoulder.

"Officer Webber" began the irritated guard, who had been calling after Westfield the length of the corridor.

Westfield turned with a start, but kept a foot breaching the exit.

"The Führer has requested to speak with you, immediately" continued the guard.

Westfield stood for a moment; the guard had no gun to hand and had released his grip on Westfield; running for the door was a possibility. He blankly saw the guards mouth move in slow speech movements, the oscillations of his throat as he repeated the request. *Or, this could be the opportunity.* The muted bass tones emanating from the clean shaven guard quickly snapped back into focus, emerging from the background to strike Westfield's ear drums with sharpness and clarity.

"Sorry" Westfield started, his voice cracking slightly. He cleared his throat and quickly continued "I'm a little distant this evening. Long journey today. Please, lead the way. I'd be honoured to speak with the Führer".

He took a chance on the opportunity laid before him.

***

Myers found as good a vantage point as he could hope; slightly elevated, tree cover, far enough from Berghoff to blend in with his surroundings, but close enough for any targets to be a sure shot. His blinks were becoming exaggerated as his fatigue spiralled, making assembly of his silenced sniper rifle arduous.

Lying on his front, rifle by his side, he looked out towards the front corner of the pale building, digging the eye pieces of the binoculars into the soft flesh around his eyes to force himself awake.

He watched as Westfield emerged, his whole body suddenly alert, muscles taught with the surging adrenaline. He stared on, unblinking with apprehension, as a tendril-like hand emerged and enveloped the shoulder of Westfield.

Still looking ahead, he reached for his rifle; the clawing fibres of the fabric blanket on which the rifle had been laid could not keep their grip on the smooth metallic contours as Myers dragged it towards him. He loaded the weapon and positioned the stock against his shoulder.

Ready.

FIFTEEN

"Adolf Hitler sprechen…"

A message was relayed down the phone line. His tight eyelids scraped open in a single tired effort as his rich brown eyes dilated, opening like chasmal voids, drawing in the desperately retreating light.

The passage of a moment lapsed for just a moment, before the order was given for the guest to be shown through.

The handset was replaced with an authoritative clap as the Bakelite parts collided and he turned on his heels, unhurriedly, and made for the supple leather of his chair. The sun had finished the latter part of its skyward journey; the discarded orange hue of the evening, which had settled across the mountainous landscape to highlight the soft curves of the distant, snowy ground, the angular facets of the exposed rock, and the linear limbs of the trees, had been pushed aside by the encroaching inky night.

He sank back into his chair and made a hard leer at the diminishing flames in the fireplace, his lips pursed together and the bridge of his nose pursed in musing.   He stared blankly at the fire, whose dance was slowing in pace and fading in vibrancy. The crown of the obedient Alsatian was gently toyed in a rhythmic wave-like motion. Occasionally the pedigree dog would look up at its master with woeful eyes as brown as the weathered bark on the alpine trees beyond the large glass window occupying the right-hand wall of the room.

A few minutes passed, the burnt sky somehow darkened further, complimented by the dying fire. The Alsatian took to lying afoot the hearth by the radiating embers. He shifted in his chair, the cushions exhaled as he struggled to find comfort, the leather groaned like the twisting hull of a ship.

There was a knock on the door in far corner behind the leader's throne, and like a loose gate in a maelstrom the heavy hardwood barrier was thrust open, though restrained by the opener before colliding with the bookcase, rich in faded pastel hues of countless books, which spanned the back wall of the room.

***

Westfield entered the room. The dark wood panelling seemed to absorb any of the dying light that struggled free of the flickering fireplace, forcing his eyes to strain through the gloom. There was a leathery must to the air, almost irritable to the throat. He could taste the faint hint of boot polish which hung in the stagnant atmosphere, forcing a slight involuntary grimace. Underfoot, the parquet flooring had a glasslike sheen, excessively polished by the countless people to stand just where Westfield was at that moment. The door was clicked shut behind Westfield by the guard who had chaperoned him, who proceeded to stand in front of the door, seemingly blocking the exit. But for the muted ticking of the embers, Westfield felt he was stood in an anechoic cell, no sounds permitted in or out.

Unsure of the protocol, Westfield remained stood for a moment, emulating the alpine structures lost to the gloom, before remembering his manners.

"Heil Hitler!" he barked fiercely, arm stretched upwards, before resuming his motionless stance. On throwing down his arm from the salute, the blood rushing back to his hand and reinstated the throbbing; a soft beading of sweat began to grow across his forehead, with occasional runs downward towards his clenched chin.

The lethargic passage of time was becoming increasingly vexatious; a stalemate of silence, although only one person could break it. Westfield made furtive glances around the room, so brief his minds-eyes could only replicate blurred lines of features, coloured with muted hues from a limited palette.

With shattering relief, the silence was broken by a hoarse voice.

"I'm tired of being caged in here. I want some air" spoke Hitler, to no one in particular, his gaze unwavering into the middle distance. It was implied all personnel in the room were to follow the Führer outside, despite not being directly asked.

This is perfect! thought Westfield; he no longer needed a ropey excuse to try and lure him outside and into the crosshairs of Myers.

Hitler moved across from the far side of the room, his slightly hunched form looking somewhat sinister, silhouetted against the ebbing embers in the fireplace. He stopped and looked directly into Westfield's eyes; the corners of his eyes tightened almost imperceptibly, followed by an equally subtle nod before he continued for the exit. The heavy, solid wood door was opened hastily by the guard and the threshold crossed by the villainous figure.

Westfield snapped himself from his incredulity and made after the Führer, avoiding eye contact with the guard still holding open the door. Unsure exactly how to walk with the leader of Germany, he ensured his maximum walking speed allowed him to maintain a safe gap behind the Führer.

The disjointed party approached the front of Berghof. The stage of the outside terrace was so tantalisingly close Westfield could almost taste the metallic blood as the copper jacketed bullet tumbled clumsily through the right temple, jetting a warm mist over surroundings, catching people full in the face before their reflexive withdrawal from the eruption. A second bullet would promptly follow, before the already deceased had hit the floor, punching effortlessly through a lung before shattering a rib bone as it exited the falling form. There may even be a third shot, fired in the adrenaline fuelled drama of the occasion, just grazing the body as it lifelessly twists out of the trajectory, the hot metal undeformed until the moment its halted by the brickwork of the front façade, a small puff of dust, unnoticed against the backdrop of events, emanating momentarily from the final resting place of the contorted lead.

***

"I understand your vehicle has suffered some damage, Frederick" Hitler had paused as the double front doors were opened by two guards; although addressing Westfield behind him, he had only turned his gaze slightly, keeping his body directed squarely ahead.

Shit! Westfield panicked. All he needed was to force a few more paces out of Hitler, just a few more. *Everything is so close!*

Westfield kept walking, towards Hitler and towards the salvation of the exit. He had only just become aware of the two or three additional guards now behind him; he couldn't be sure of numbers without an incriminatingly obvious leer behind him.

"Ah. Yes" started Westfield, stretching out the syllables to buy him precious seconds to think "A jealous ex-husband of my girlfriend unfortunately" he left it there, wanting to keep the explanation vague to avoid tripping over his own lies.

Westfield continued to the open front doors, acting as casually as he could.

"He's no longer of worry, mind you. Him, or his bastard *Jew* associates" he spat the religious emphasis, playing to appease his audience.

"The evening air is fantastic here" Westfield nonchalantly uttered, seemingly shrugging off the anti-Semitic remarks as everyday comments.

He stepped through the doors, past the guards and out onto the terrace. He feigned absorbing the view from all directions, but gave a very slight nod when facing the direction of Myers.

"Does not every man dream for this view?" Westfield continued, trying to lure the beast from its lair.

Hitler started forward. Westfield's eyes widened, his pulse quickened, his throat raw as he tried to swallow; his body tensed in apprehension of the impending shot, the shockwave slapping him on the chest before he felt any of the fallout.

***

The Führer continued to walk towards Westfield. No shots resounded. No blood spattered. No bodies fell.

"Something wrong, Weber" Hitler spoke as he passed Westfield, heading for the low balcony at the perimeter of the terrace.

"No, not at all my Führer. Why do you ask?" he asked, immediately regretful. He turned to walk towards Hitler, the movements granting camouflage as he reached into his coat pocket to clutch the plundered breakfast knife. He bit the inside of his cheek as he forced, willed, the tender flesh of his swollen hand to grasp the blunt instrument. Westfield joined Hitler adjacent to the balcony.

"I'm curious" Hitler spoke, in a slow, cryptic manner "your oppressive cough, I can't help but notice you appear cured".

SHIT! Westfield panicked once again. There was no way he could have known his alter ego should have a terminal lung condition. He'd given himself away as soon as he'd approached the building. He glanced to the front of the building, the guards materialising at the entrance and down the hallway, poised to file out like ants from a kicked nest once instructed.

There was a soft glow from the lifeless windows of Berghof; slight height differences in adjacent tiles draped long shadows across the terrace, seemingly creating spear-like arrows, aimed at Westfield. He noticed for the first time the small swarm of gnats, which had migrated from the alluring light of the windows to the more inviting flesh of Westfield. He didn't bother trying to swat away the sensation.

A pop and a splutter was heard, complimented by twisting metal.

***

Myers saw a figure emerge from the shafts of lights clawing outwards from the front of the building. Switching from his naked, tired eye to the rifle scope, he saw Westfield, looking in his vague direction. A small nod; Hitler was nearby.

Myers cocked his rifle, restraining himself to do so slowly to reduce the metallic clank associated with a bullet being thrust into the barrel.

Then he emerged. Hitler. Perfectly clear line of sight.

Myers was immediately fully alert. He drew a short breath, glowered down the scope and positioned his crosshairs over the left temple of his target. With a degree of finesse he smoothly pulled the trigger.

Nothing. No click, even. The rifle was jammed.

He retracted his head in consternation, sat up on his knees and looked over the rifle, rolling it over and over in his hands with no real direction or clue for what he was in search of.

Damaged in the landing?

Whatever the issue, he had no time to correct the rifle. He thought for a brief moment, looked back down the scope of the rifle to assess the surroundings, to search for any usable features. Hitler was on the move towards Westfield. There was no time to spare.

He detached the scope from the rifle, retrieved a stored pistol from his pack and, in a crouched run, made his way down the embankment he'd been on and towards the closest side of Berghof to Myers, where visitor cars had been parked in an orderly fashion.

Within the cover of the shadows, Myers crouched over a polished bonnet, which seemed to sparkle with the faintest of reflected light rays, and took stock of the present situation with the scope; he watched a magnified image of Westfield wince as his hand seemed to lock onto something in his coat pocket, whilst moving towards where Hitler now stood against a section of balustrade lining the terrace.

He pocketed the scope and hastily found the vehicle with the tell-tale smashed side window; reaching in, he found Westfield hadn't forgotten to leave the keys under the sun visor. With a cough from the engine, the car popped and spluttered to life, the thin haze of exhaust fumes chugging haphazardly into the gloom.

Myers released the handbrake, crunched the vehicle into gear and set the car in motion to roll across the edge of the terrace. With a slow crunch of twisting metal, the car stalled to a halt when it collided with a tree, level with the balcony of the terrace.

***

The internal combustive pops of an engine were heard. All parties looked across to the far side of the terrace, where a black car, the hard lines of its features smudged with the light starved background, rolled out and along the edge of the terrace before crunching into a tree. The low speed impact twisted the chrome bumper into a lacklustre hug of the tree. The engine coughed to a stop, and all fell still and silent; even the gentle winds and eddy currents held their breath momentarily.

With frustrated gesticulation, Hitler tuned to the guards and signalled for the incident to be investigated.

So baffled himself, Westfield faltered slightly before feeling the knife in his hand. He drew it from his pocket, the small serrations on the blade snagging on the bobbled fabric.

He took a step forward, his free hand pinning the shoulder of his foe, and drove the knife into Hitler's side, just below the ribcage; the mirrored stainless steel reflected the snarling anguish on his face, before the image was blotted out by the warm, viscous liquid flowing along the cool steel. Westfield's hand erupted in pain; the handle dug through his gloved hand to the raw flesh below, which was easily torn having been softened by persistent perspiration. His grip involuntarily relaxed on the knife. He was done

***

Myers heard the rattle of gunfire, like stones dropping onto metal washboards, and braced himself. He instinctively ducked and curled himself into as small a target as possible. But no projectiles flitted by him.

He heard German shouts and the tinny reloading of weapons, metallic footsteps as boots caught the spent bullet casings underfoot.

A face appeared at a side window of the vehicle, the expression alerted by the sight of Myers laid across the rear footwell. Pistol already in-hand, Myers let loose a single round which penetrated the eye socket of the German, flicking back the head in a swift movement before the entire body fell forward, through the spider-webbed glass, becoming caught in a sprawled heap, half-in the car.

Myers wrestled himself free from the confined space and peered past the deceased passenger to see Westfield slumped at the base of the balustrade, colour spreading across the heavy cotton uniform as if it were blotting paper. There was Hitler, a knife protruding clearly from his side.

The raining of gunfire broke Myers' incredulous stare. He writhed his way between the front seats to fall into the driver's seat. Staying hunched, he twisted the key and closed his eyes as the engine cranked and cranked. Bullets pierced the front passenger door, small puffs of dust being thumped from the carpet as the spiralling projectiles thwacked into the footwell. The holes torn in the door were illuminated in a random fashion by the spits of flame from the assault rifles, like twinkling stars on a clear night. Line of sight between the driver's seat and terrace was broken by the German slumped over the rear passenger door, who took as much fire as the rest of the vehicle, the corpse shuddering slightly with each hit; occasional spits of blood flew forward, clumsily catching Myers on the ear or showering the plastic heater controls.

The car lethargically throbbed to life. Myers slammed the gearstick into reverse and dabbed the throttle, freeing the front bumper from the knobbly clutches of the tree in front. With a notchy interaction with the gearstick, he found first gear and leaned all his weight on the accelerator. Bullets continued to zip through the dust screen kicked up by the skidding rear wheels, tiny vortexes being punched in the haze before dusty fingers reached across to repair the gap.

Myers kept himself as low as possible, his head barely above the top of the steering wheel. A rear tyre was shot, forcing Myers to fight for control of the squirming tail of the car; the dead soldier hanging over the rear door was tossed like a ragdoll by a frustrated child, the legs flailing as though in a slow motion run, the tips of his boots just kissing the ground.

A barrage of automatic gunfire rained down from the Germans pursuing on foot; the rear of the car was riddled, the rear window smashed, the taillights non-existent, paint blistered around the wounds in the steel panels. A bullet wormed its way through a veil of dust, silver in the non-light between dusk and night, over the ripped tops of the rear seats, through the side of the driver's seat, spitting white stuffing, and into the right shoulder of Myers. Involuntarily he yanked at the steering the wheel, sending the car into a spin he couldn't recover. The vehicle came to halt, sideways, the driver's side facing back towards Berghof.

Being so open to attack left Myers with no choice but to exit the vehicle. He clambered across the gearstick and passenger seat and clawed at the interior door handle, falling out of the vehicle onto the dry dirt track before rushing to take cover behind the body still hanging from the rear door. Over the deafening claps reverberating around the vehicle, Myers could just make out the crunch of stones under galloping boots, drawing nearer and nearer.

Fighting back the onset of resignation, he pivoted in his crouched position, his eyes straining to survey the silhouetted gloom. The sparkle of gunfire made the trees blink and the rocky outcrop shiver.

His head whipped back round to the car as the thought ignited. He frantically searched his pockets for the Swiss army knife, pulled open the blade and reached under the rear of the car. He stabbed the tool repeatedly into the fuel tank; the flammable liquid glugged out, ran across his hand and pooled on the ground. His sleeve drew the cold liquid slowly up his forearm.

He scrambled into the front of the vehicle and pressed the smooth Bakelite cigarette lighter, before retreating and anxiously awaiting the soft click as the heating element popped up from its housing.

Another tyre burst and the front corner of the car sagged. Bullets continued to beat down like torrential rain on a thin metal roof. The shouts from the guards were close. Too close.

A guard materialised at the driver side of the car, weapon brandished like an extension of his limbs. Myers threw the penknife, which did little more than force a momentary step back from the guard. There was a soft pop. His eyes darted.

The lighter!

Myers lunged into the cabin and yanked the lighter free. The fuel vapour soaked into his sleeve ignited. He threw himself back from the car in frenzy at the same moment the guard opened fire, drilling holes into the dashboard with a quick burst of flames. The cigarette lighter flew from his burning grip.

Instinctively, Myers rolled on the ground in attempt to extinguish the flames. His burning flesh caught the edge of the pooled fuel under the car, setting the rear of the vehicle immediately ablaze in a roaring yellow heat. He stood to move away, shaking free the burning jacket in the process. He patted his arm frantically to choke the residual flames on his hand as he began to run down the track, preying the conflagrant obstacle would act to grant him safe passage.

***

Something hit the guards chest, and he took a small step back, instinctively twisting away from the direction of the projectile. He was taken aback as flames crawled their way up the arm of the figure reaching into the front of the car. He raised his weapon and let loose three short bursts, splintering the interior into sharp fragments of confetti. The flames had fallen to the other side of the vehicle, flickering wildly. Confident he had neutralised the foe, he reloaded his weapon as other guards finally caught up to vehicle, their lungs clawing at the humid air, chokingly thick with gunpowder and the faintly acrid smell of fuel.

With a wheezed whoosh, the rear of the vehicle was alight; the group retracted slightly from the heat and shielded themselves from the intense light, their eyes having adjusted to the inky gloom. They collectively navigated the sloping treeline edging the driveway, detouring from the blaze, before bursting back onto the track like ants from a stricken nest. The increasing numbers quickly resulted in a single jagged silhouetted mass against the burning backdrop. Their vision now impaired for seeing through the curtain of darkness, they opened fire aimlessly down the curving track. Bullets zipped between the tress and the rock face, shattering layers of bark and splintering chunks of stone, which fell to the ground together in a contrasting shower of dark and light, supple and brittle.

***

Helped to his feet, hand pressed to his side to stem the blood flow, Hitler glared briefly down the track away from Berghof. The long sweep of the drive through the trees prevented him witnessing unfolding events, although the crackle of gunfire did ping back and forth between the mountains and woodland, echoing round his ears like a disorderly symphony. Features emerged from the charcoal gloom, highlighted by a flitting orange glow which made the distant trees sway and rock faces wink.

Hitler turned towards the front of Berghof, his upper lip pursed and brow furrowed. The sepia of his cold eyes was just picked out by the electric lights of the building, casting out their hue like discarded straw. He turned to the high ranking officer that had come to offer his aid, looked him so hard in the eyes the officer blinked.

"I want him found" his teeth gritted as he finished the order.

He made his way back into his sanctuary, obedient personnel flocking around the Führer like bees around a hive.

SIXTEEN

The twin huts for the gatehouse stood beneath tall lampposts, swathed in artificial light which falsified the colours of reality. The sodium lamps burned with a faint hiss, their orange cones of light picked out by the infinitesimal particulates suspended in the air, gently drifting unavailingly. Moths repeatedly crashed into the thin glass encasing the filaments, the tiniest of rings drowned out by the flutter of paper-like wings.

They sat squat against the absolute darkness of the alpine evening, the thin laths cladding the exterior doing little to fend off the icy clutches of the night, the small bars of the electric fire burning fiercely, futilely.

At the crackle of gunfire, two chairs screeched across the wooden flooring. The two guards exited the small building with haste and stepped beyond the threshold of the orange cones, allowing their eyes to adjust to the gloom up the track. With a silent glance at each other, one of the men retreated back to the hut to pick up the red handset, a direct line to Berghof. Mere seconds passed before the handset with thrust back down, a shadow-like handprint being left in the thin layer of dust on the receiver.

He skidded back outside and relayed the keywords of the message; *Imposter. Assassination attempt. Dead or alive.*

Round the long sweep of the track, a man in German officer uniform emerged, running, his one hand pressed into his opposite shoulder and shrouded in blood. The guards raised their rifles in unison, and in a synchronised and rehearsed fashion, coldly let loose flickering spits of lead.

The imposter fell to the ground, but almost as quickly rolled into the adjacent treeline. The guards robotically started down the track. They came to a reddened, sticky patch on the dusty ground. *New or existing wound?*

The trees danced their endless, rhythmically slow waltz, the alluring movements detracting attention; the wind sang through the branches, the notes subtle but so clear as to command full attention; the soft snapping of a branch seemed almost out of place in the symphony.

Printed in Great Britain
by Amazon